*Boo*

MW01200036

**Audiobooks by April Wilson**

For links to my audiobooks, please visit my website:
www.aprilwilsonauthor.com/audiobooks

Copyright © 2019 by April E. Barnswell/Wilson Publishing LLC

Cover by Steamy Designs

Wilson Publishing
P.O. Box 292913
Dayton, OH 45429
www.aprilwilsonauthor.com

Visit www.aprilwilsonauthor.com to sign up for the author's e-mail newsletter to be notified about upcoming releases.

ISBN: 9781797009803

Published in the United States of America
First Printing February 2019

# Marry Me

McIntyre Security Bodyguard Series
Book 9

APRIL WILSON

# Dedication

For Lia and Jonah, who are perfect together.

# 1

## Lia McIntyre

One of my favorite places to hang out these days is on the black leather armchair in front of the console in my boyfriend's recording studio. I've got my scruffy boots propped up on the console and an ice-cold Pepsi in my hand as I kick back and watch my guy do his thing.

*Jonah Locke.*

*Damn.*

*That man makes my girl parts tingle.*

And the amazing thing is... he's mine. All mine.

Jonah Locke, as in former lead singer of the band *Locke.* Now he's a rebel—my kind of guy—having left his big L.A. record label and struck out on his own. He considers himself an indie singer/song-writer, and he writes, performs, records, and distributes his own work.

I'm so damn proud of him. He told that asshat of a manager of his—Dwight Peterson—to *shove* it. Thank God. I couldn't stand the man. He's a weasel—and in calling him that, I am offending real weasels everywhere.

I could sit here all day and watch Jonah strumming chords and picking out notes on his guitar. The man is ridiculously hot. And his voice! *Oh, my God.* There's a reason why there are about three dozen screaming girls hanging out in the parking lot of this recording studio—all hoping for the chance to catch a glimpse of *the* Jonah Locke.

Jonah leans forward to jot something down in his notebook, which is propped up in front of him on a music stand. His expression is a mask of concentration as he's caught up in his songwriting. The man has skills coming out his ears. He even wrote a song *for me* when we first met and performed it live at a local pub.

He just happens to lift his face and catch me staring at him. He smiles, his dark eyes missing nothing, and my belly does a little flip. Because... *damn.* That man. Fortunately, he doesn't realize how appealing he is, and so he doesn't have a big head.

I honestly don't know how I ended up with this guy... one of America's favorite musical heart-throbs. When he and his band came to Chicago to work on a new album, his manager—that asshat Dwight—hired my brother's company to provide personal protection for Jonah. Jonah needed a bodyguard because his enthusiastic fans followed him everywhere. The man couldn't even cross the street without garnering a crowd.

My CEO brother—Shane—picked yours truly to cover Jonah's very fine ass. Shane thought Jonah and I would hit it off well. He was right.

It made total sense for the both of us when Jonah ended up leaving the band and striking out on his own. We're both introverts, hating crowds and the spotlight. We both keep low profiles, preferring to stay home and hang out together. Now Jonah plays primarily small venues, local pubs that can't seat more than a couple hundred people. He plans events at the last minute in order to keep the crowds small. Even then, I have to arrange for an entire team of security to help manage the events and keep the venues from being stormed.

Jonah frowns as he scratches something out on his notebook. Then he strums a few chords and sings a few words before writing something down.

I love to watch him work. I love the way he bites his lower lip as he concentrates, the way his forehead wrinkles when he frowns. The way his dark eyes light up when he catches me watching him, and the way he watches me right back.

Jonah's way too good for me; I realize that. But for some inexplicable reason, he loves me too. Frankly, I don't get it. I'm far more trouble than I'm worth.

And now I can't imagine my life without him.

He's released half a dozen songs since going it alone—all have hit the number one spot on the music charts. One of them is riding high on the top ten chart right now, and another two are in the top twenty. And the radio stations love Jonah. He's down-to-Earth, he's approachable, and he's grateful for the publicity he gets.

Right now he's working on the melody for a new song. It's a love song, something slow and mushy. For some reason, ever since we met, he's been gravitating toward love songs. Go figure.

The lights in the recording studio are turned down low, creating an intimate atmosphere. There's a single spotlight focused on the music stand in front of Jonah. He stops strumming his guitar to scribble some notes on the sheet music. I stare, mesmerized at the sight of him.

His skin is perpetually sun-kissed, golden and tawny. His long, dark hair is twisted up neatly into a manbun, and his short, trim beard frames a strong jaw. When he sings, I can't help staring at his lips, so sinfully beautiful as they form each word. His voice is low, with a rough quality that makes me weak in the knees.

I know only too well what those lips feel like on my skin, on every inch of my body.

*Damn.*

The longer I sit here watching him, the more I find myself squirming in my chair. He's an amazing and generous lover, and watching him work makes me think of sex. I imagine walking into the recording booth, like I've done on numerous occasions, stalking him like a panther. When he sees me coming, he'll sit up straight on his barstool and watch me approach. His expression will darken with arousal and his chest will rise and fall with anticipation. I think we've had almost as much sex here in the recording studio as we've had in our apartment.

Okay, I can't just sit here getting all hot and bothered... not while he has work to do. I shoot up out of my chair, waving to him as he watches my movements, and head to the adjoining room where I have set up a small workout room. I've got a treadmill in here, a free-standing weight machine, and a punching bag suspended from the ceiling for those days when I feel the need to hit something—which is usually every day.

I remove my short boots and strip out of my jeans and T-shirt to pull on black biker shorts, a black tank top, and running shoes. Then I fire up the treadmill. I try to run at least six miles every day to keep up my endurance. And I run *hard*.

The treadmill is programmed to take me from a brief warm-up to a full six-mile run on varying inclines, to a brief cool down. Technically, I'm on duty as Jonah's bodyguard, but since this is a private recording studio now, and fully secured, no one comes or goes without our knowledge and permission. Jonah's safe in here, even without me hovering over him every second. If anyone were to break in, the security system would alert everyone who needs to know. So, while there could be anywhere from two dozen to two hundred fans lurking outside the rear exit, waiting for a chance to get a peek at Jonah as he comes and goes, he's quite safe in here.

As I run, I can easily see the bank of monitors displaying what the surveillance cameras see outside the building, in the parking lot, and even in the recording studio control room. The only space that isn't under surveillance is the actual sound booth, where Jonah sits on his barstool strumming his guitar and writing his next big hit.

It doesn't take me long to run six miles, because I push myself. I'm always pushing myself. At my height, I can't say that my size is an advantage—especially when I'm going up against a male opponent who towers over me and outweighs me by a hundred pounds. But I'm mean as hell and I hit hard. And I prefer to handle situations without brandishing weapons.

As Jonah Locke's bodyguard, I can keep him safe from all those hysterical fans who want to slobber all over him, rip off a piece of his clothing as a souvenir, and have his baby. *Nope. Not going to happen. Not on my watch.*

After my run, I do some cool down stretches. Then I slip on a pair of boxing gloves and go a few rounds with the punching bag, working on my reflexes. Plus, I just like hitting things. It helps quiet the noise that's perpetually swirling around in my head.

*I'm complicated.* That's how Jonah puts it.

But let's be honest... I'm a pain in the ass. Why sugar coat it? In my family, as the youngest of seven kids, I'm the outlier. I'm the one who doesn't fit in. Even my sister Hannah, who traipses around the wilderness studying wolves, is better adjusted to being with people than I am.

And still, despite my *complications*, Jonah hasn't run away screaming.

*At least not yet.*

* * *

After I work out, I change back into my street clothes. I need a shower, but I'll wait until we get home. We do have a bath with a shower here at the studio, but I don't feel comfortable leaving him completely unprotected while I'm in the shower, out of ear shot. I don't want to push my luck.

According to the surveillance cameras focused on the rear parking lot and the back entrance to the building, there are approximately three dozen fan girls lurking outside right now, waiting for a chance to lay their eyes on Jonah. They're mostly young girls, middle school and high school age, so they probably don't pose much of a threat. Sometimes, though, it gets ugly when they attempt to grab him in the hopes of tearing off a piece of his clothing. I'll be damned if I'll let someone actually touch him.

I head back into the control room and glance at the clock on the wall. It's four o'clock. We usually head out around four, unless he's in the middle of something and wants to keep at it a while longer. Right now he looks pretty engrossed in whatever he's doing, so I sit back and relax and enjoy the scenery. I don't want to rush him. He's more than generous and patient with his time where I'm concerned, so I'm happy to return the favor.

He runs through a series of chords on the guitar, making notations in his notebook. Then he sets down his pencil and leans over the guitar, teasing out some notes before he plays a few stanzas.

*Damn. That sounds good.*

My phone chimes with an incoming Google alert, and I see that someone posted on social media that Jonah is here at the studio. *Great!* Now watch the fans flood in.

Whenever someone posts an actual sighting of Jonah, the crowds swell. *Crap.* We need to leave. I can only hold back so many eager fans on my own. Pulling my semi-automatic on a bunch of teenagers is not cool.

I open the door to the soundproof room and lean against the door jamb, my arms crossed over my chest.

Jonah glances up from his work and checks the time on his chunky wrist watch. He's one of the few people I know who still wears a watch. He smiles. "Hey, tiger. Time to go?"

*Tiger.* He came up with *tiger* as a nickname for me because he said he was afraid I'd hit him if he called me *pumpkin* or *baby.* He was right.

"Sorry, pal," I say, walking toward him, "but someone just blabbed your whereabouts on social media. We should take off before the crowd size gets out of hand."

Jonah sets his guitar on its stand beside his stool. "No problem. I'm ready." He snags my hand and pulls me close, between his knees.

I'm close enough that I can feel the heat of his body and smell him, a tantalizing mix of faint cologne, soap, and warm male. *God, he smells good.* So good I want to wrap myself up in him.

He wraps his hand behind my neck. "You're sweating. Did you run?"

"Yes, so don't get too close. I need a shower."

Grinning, he leans forward and kisses me anyway, his lips coaxing mine to respond. "You could be covered head to toe in mud, and I'd still want you."

I roll my eyes and tug him off his stool. "Come on, Romeo. Let's pack up and head home."

We shut down the recording equipment and turn off the lights before heading down the central hallway to the rear exit. I reach for my compact semi-automatic, which I keep tucked in a holster at my lower back. I pop out the magazine and check the rounds, then pop the magazine back in and tuck the gun in my holster.

There are surveillance monitors at the rear door, too, showing what's waiting for us outside before we open the solid metal door. "I'll push them back," I tell him, mentally estimating the crowd size. It's manageable. "You make a run for the Jeep."

Studying the monitors, he frowns. "I think we should stay together."

I shake my head, watching the pushing and shoving increase as the crowd size grows. The Jeep is parked ten yards from the rear door, facing out to allow for a quick getaway. But right now, both the exit and our vehicle are boxed in by the crowd. "Make for the driver's seat," I tell him, sticking to my original plan.

He looks at me. "Why?"

I almost always drive, so I'm not surprised that my comment has thrown him. "The Jeep's penned in. I'll have to clear a path for you to drive through them. Once you get past the worst of it, I'll hop in."

"Lia, I'm not driving away with you out in this crowd. No way."

"Yes, you will. Unless you want me to run over a dozen of your most devoted fans?"

He scowls, sighing heavily. "I don't like this."

"I know you don't, rock star." I go up on my toes to kiss him. "But you have to let me do my job…. Unless you want a new bodyguard."

He pulls me into his arms, resting his chin on the top of my head.

"That's not funny. You know I don't."

"Then stick with the plan. I'll open the door and push them back. You make a run for the driver's door. I'll hold them off you. Easy peasy. All right?"

He glares at me, far from all right with the plan. But we really don't have any other options unless we care to call for back-up. Personally, I don't think the situation calls for it.

"All right, fine," he says. "But I swear to God, if you get hurt—"

"I'm not going to get hurt." I reach for the door knob. "Ready? On my mark...three, two, one, go!"

I push the door open, putting all my weight into it so it swings wide. I step outside, positioning myself between Jonah and the girls, my arms splayed wide to keep them from rushing him. The screaming intensifies, and they try to press closer. Camera flashes are going off like fireworks, nearly blinding me. The shouting is deafening as they all call Jonah's name.

"Go!" I tell him, and he slips out behind me and walks quickly along the rear of the building toward my Jeep. I keep pace with him, forming a barrier between him and his rabid fans. Most of the girls are respectful enough to stay out of my personal space, but a few get close enough that I have to push them back.

Jonah reaches the driver's door and I hear the tell-tale beep of the locks disengaging. He slips behind the wheel and shuts his door, locking the vehicle once more. I slide to the front of the vehicle to begin clearing the way for him to pull out of the parking spot.

These girls are pretty harmless. I don't think any of them is a real threat to Jonah's safety, but the sheer numbers of them creates a problem. If he gets boxed in, even well-meaning fans can create serious safety issues.

I herd them away from the vehicle, mostly in an effort to prevent their toes from being run over. They shift back, stumbling and knocking into each other, and I manage to get a few feet of open space between them and the Jeep. "Come on, ladies, back it up! Let the poor guy go home to his dinner."

By this time, there are at least fifty phones in the air as the girls— and a few guys—take pictures and record video, hoping to get a glimpse of Jonah. The Jeep windows are darkly tinted, so now that he's safely in the vehicle, he's out of range of the cameras.

Jonah lowers his window a bit. "Lia, get in the vehicle!"

"Not yet!" I push the girls farther back, creating an opening for Jonah to inch the Jeep out of the spot. I move to the front of the vehicle, and he keeps pace with me, heading toward the parking lot exit.

Once we're almost clear to the exit, I jog around the front of the vehicle to the passenger seat. Jonah pops the locks in time for me to open the door and hop in. After slamming the door shut and locking it, I lean back in my seat with a relieved sigh. Mission accomplished.

"Put your seatbelt on," Jonah says, sounding far from happy.

I buckle myself in as he creeps toward the street. Once we're free of the parking lot and can drive away at a reasonable speed, the crowd melts back.

I stretch my back and arms. "That was fun." Now that he's out of the fray, I can relax.

Jonah throws me a strained look—he's clearly still not amused.

"Too soon?" I ask him, reaching behind me to withdraw my handgun from my back holster. I slip the gun into the glove box and close the door.

# 2

## *Lia McIntyre*

These crowds are getting out of hand," Jonah says as he picks up speed on the already crowded Chicago streets. "It's too much for just one person to manage."

I study his profile—his jaws clenched, posture rigid, hands white-knuckling the steering wheel. His beautiful lips are pressed into a flat line, and there's a muscle ticking in his cheek. *Yeah, he's not happy.*

A lump forms in my belly.

We're both silent for the rest of the drive home. Our apartment building is located on Lake Shore Drive in the Gold Coast, just a fifteen-minute drive from the recording studio. Jonah pulls the Jeep into the underground garage and parks in our assigned spot, not far from the bank of elevators.

He jumps out of the Jeep and waits for me to join him. The longer he's silent, the bigger the lump grows in my belly.

*He's not happy.*

And when Jonah's not happy, I get scared.

As long as we've been dating, I've had this fear in the back of my mind that one day he'll grow dissatisfied with me. One day, he'll wake up and realize I'm not enough. And then he'll want out.

I never wanted to date anyone. I never wanted to commit to someone and risk getting hurt. Risk rejection. Jonah pushed me into it, and because I was so crazy about him, I gave in. We've been together for nearly two years now, sharing my apartment, and we've been happy. At least I thought so. And no one is more surprised about it than I am. Honestly, I never expected it to last more than a few months. Two years? Sheesh. We're practically an old married couple.

Only we're not married.

And not for lack of trying on Jonah's part. I think he's proposed to me seven times so far, and each time I change the subject.

The elevator door opens, and we step into the empty car, standing side by side. I push the button to our floor, and the elevator doors whoosh shut.

As we ascend, I risk a glance at Jonah's profile. He's still grinding his teeth, obviously still upset. The longer he stews, the more anxious I feel. "Just say it, Jonah. Whatever's bothering you... just get it off your chest."

He turns to me. "We can't keep going on like this."

The bottom falls out of my stomach, and I feel sick. I take a deep breath, stealing myself for the inevitable pain. I've known this was coming. It shouldn't come as a surprise. But damn, it hurts. My eyes prick as tears start to form. *Don't fucking let him see you cry!*

"Fine," I say, when the elevator doors open on our floor. I step out of the car and hustle down the hall to our apartment. I've got the door open and I'm inside before him.

"Lia, wait!"

*No.* I'm not going to stand around and wait for him to tell me this isn't working. That it's not enough. I head into the bathroom, lock the door, and turn on the shower. While the water heats, I strip naked, avoiding my own reflection in the mirror. I know what I'll see. Red, teary eyes. Pain-filled eyes.

*Why did I do this to myself? Why did I allow myself to fall in love with him?* I should have known it wouldn't last. And now... shit, I'll be lost without him. He's my best friend, my lover... my everything.

I grab a washcloth and toss a clean towel over the shower curtain rod. Then I step into the shower, letting the hot water pelt me. As I reach for the soap, I hear him knocking.

He tries the doorknob, but it's locked. He knocks again. "Lia?"

"I'm busy!"

Pain and sorrow well up inside me, and I set down the bar of soap. My throat is so tight it hurts, and my heart is pounding. I draw in a shaky breath and try to rein in my panic, but I'm quickly losing the battle.

When the tears start flowing, I close my eyes and hold my face under the water. I swallow my sobs, biting my lips until they hurt, and cry silently as the water washes the tears away.

A moment later, I feel a cool draft of air as the shower curtain is pulled back. I turn to look just as Jonah steps into the shower, naked. He picked the lock—the bastard.

When he sees that I'm crying, his expression falls, and he reaches for me, pulling me into his arms.

"Jesus, Lia," he murmurs against my forehead. "Talk to me. What's wrong?"

My throat is so tight I don't trust myself to speak. I'm afraid I'll lose it completely.

When I don't answer him, he pulls back and looks me in the eye, his warm hands framing my face. "Tell me what's wrong."

"Nothing."

His expression clearly says *give-me-a-break*. "Try again."

"You said... we can't go on like this."

He looks perplexed. "So? We really pushed it this afternoon. Things could have gotten ugly out there." He shakes his head. "It has to stop. I'm not going to risk you getting hurt."

Now it's my turn to be perplexed. "You meant the crowd?"

"Of course I meant the crowd. What did you think I meant?" He searches my gaze as if trying to decipher my thoughts. When I don't answer him, he takes hold of my shoulders and makes me look at him. "Lia, tell me. What did you think I meant?"

"I thought you meant...*us*."

He looks dumbfounded. "Jesus, Lia. How could you think that?"

Jonah pulls me close again, this time wrapping his arms around me and holding me to his chest. He leans down and kisses the side of my neck. "You know I love you."

I pull out of his grasp. "Yeah, well people fall *out* of love all the time. Why do you think the divorce rate is so high?"

Jonah shakes his head as he grabs the soap and quickly lathers his hands. Then he hands the soap to me. We wash quickly and rinse off. Then he turns off the water and hands me the towel hanging over the curtain rod.

He steps out of the shower and grabs a clean towel for himself, briskly drying off. Then, without saying a word, he sweeps me up into his arms and carries me to our bedroom, laying me down in the middle of the unmade bed.

He joins me on the bed, covering us both to stave off the chill. "We need to talk."

Those dreaded four words make my heart start hammering. He draws me into his arms, against his hot, damp body.

He turns me to face him and rubs my back. He's silent for the longest time, and that does nothing to lower my anxiety. This is why I prefer to be single. *No doubts. No fears.*

Finally, he speaks, holding my gaze. "When I said we couldn't go on like this, I meant the security situation. The crowds keep getting bigger. It's more than you can handle safely on your own."

I allow myself to take a deep breath, reminding myself he's talking about security, not about our relationship. He's not breaking up with me.

The knot in my stomach slowly begins to loosen. Shit, I can handle security issues. If that's all that's bothering him...

"You could have gotten hurt this afternoon," he says, brushing his hand over my hair as he gazes down at me. *He was worried.*

I don't want him worrying about me, so I laugh off the idea. "Let a bunch of teenaged girls hurt me? That'll be the day."

"Lia, it comes down to sheer numbers. If you get swarmed by a hundred people, you could get hurt."

"I carry a gun, you know."

He gives me a look. "Sure. And you're going to pull a semi-automatic handgun on a bunch of teenage girls. You and I both know you'd never do that."

"I would if I absolutely had to."

"If my life was in danger, you might. But you wouldn't do it for yourself. It's *your* safety I'm worried about. I know you, Lia. You're the type who runs into fires, not away. If the security situation became dire, you'd risk your life for me, and I can't live with that."

My heart's still pounding because I don't know where he's going with this. "Then what do you propose?"

"I do have a proposition for you. Jake and Annie are looking at a house they're interested in buying, and they've invited us to go with them this evening to look at it. It's in a brand-new gated community. And there are plenty of lots available. I want us to go."

My eyes widen as my pulse starts racing for a whole new reason. "You want to buy a house?"

We've talked about buying a house since we started dating. Jonah wants to put a recording studio in the house so he can work from home. He's as much a homebody as I am. We're both introverts.

"Sure, I'll go. There's no harm in looking, right?"

He smiles, looking relieved. "They invited us to their place for dinner at six. After dinner, we'll go see this house they're interested in."

My brother Jake and his girlfriend, Annie, along with her adorable five-year-old son, Aiden, live in our apartment building, too, on the same floor we do. With a young child, and a baby on the way, they want to move out of the city and buy a house in the suburbs.

"Okay, fine. We'll go." I'm not sure how I feel about this talk of buying houses, but it could be worse. He could have told me that he's not happy with *me*. Finally, I can relax. My tense muscles loosen, and I sink deeper into his arms.

He turns to open the top drawer of his nightstand and pulls out a gray velvet jewelry box—the small ones. Like, ring size. He pops it open, revealing a slender gold band.

"Recognize this?" he says.

It's a plain gold band, resembling a wedding ring more than a traditional engagement ring. But there's nothing traditional about me, and he knows it. Besides, he knew I'd never wear a ring with a stone on it, or any kind of embellishment. I could actually throw a decent punch while wearing this ring.

I laugh. "Yes." Of course I do. He's shown it to me seven times before. Not that anyone's counting.

He plucks the ring from the box and holds it between us. "Give me your ring finger."

"No." And now my heart is hammering again.

"Lia, do you love me?"

"Yes."

"Are you planning to break up with me anytime soon?"

"No."

"So, you think you can stand me in your life awhile longer?"

"I guess."

"Then put on the damn ring. Maybe then you'll realize I'm serious about us."

"But it's an *engagement* ring." I'm *so* not ready for this.

"That's the plan," he says. "But if that's too much for you, we'll call it a *pre*-engagement ring. Think of it as a placeholder until you're ready for the real thing. Now give me your hand."

Jonah hovers over me, fishing beneath the bedding for my hand, and for a moment, we're playing a game of cat and mouse. I try not to laugh when he finally snags it and pulls it out from beneath the covers.

Grinning, he pries the fingers of my left hand open and slips the band on my ring finger. "The next time you doubt me—doubt what I feel for you—look at your finger, okay? This ring says 'I love you, Lia McIntyre. Forever and always.'" He grips my chin and makes me look him in the eye. "Got it?"

I stare at the slim band. *A placeholder.* Yeah, I could make this work. "Okay, fine. I'll wear it."

Jonah smiles, his dark eyes lighting up. Then he glances at the clock on the nightstand. "We're naked and in bed, and we have an hour before we have to be at your brother's place."

"Yeah? So?" I'm not going to make this easy for him. He got his way with the ring.

He presses himself against my thigh, his growing erection hot and thick. My pulse starts pounding for a whole different reason.

"We have a *whole hour,*" he says, leaning down to nuzzle the side of my neck. "I can accomplish a lot in an hour."

I shiver as he slowly trails kisses along my shoulder, then down over my clavicle. He pushes the bedding down, exposing my breasts, and I gasp when he lowers his mouth to lick one of my nipples, teasing it gently with the tip of his tongue. He draws the tip into his mouth and sucks, sending jolts of pleasure down to my core.

"Jonah!"

"Mmm?" he murmurs, not bothering to release my nipple. While he sucks on one breast, he reaches for my other, molding and shaping it with his hand. His thumb teases the tip, causing it to contract into a tight bud.

His mouth does wicked things to my breast, making my nether regions fill with aching heat. I lay my hand on the back of his head and end up petting him, while the rest of me coils up with sweet anticipation.

"Jonah, please!"

# 3

## *Lia McIntyre*

As he continues to suckle and tease my breast, heat blooms between my legs, making me wet and aching, and now I'm squirming like a live wire in his arms. *The bastard.*

His hand slips down my body to dip between my legs, his long finger sliding between the lips of my sex. I'm already wet. I can tell by how easily his finger slides along my flesh.

"Open your legs," he murmurs against my aching breast.

Needing satisfaction, and helpless to resist him, I do as he says for a change. His finger dips inside me, slowly pushing in, just a tiny bit, and then withdrawing. He repeats this over and over, dipping a little deeper each time as he lets my body's arousal coat his finger. He slides that finger in and out so slowly it drives me nuts. Then his thumb joins in the torment, stroking my clit with increasing pressure, lighting my nerve endings on fire.

My head thrashes on the pillow, and all sorts of incoherent sounds pass my lips.

He lifts his mouth from my nipple and smiles at me, looking pleased with himself. My body goes taut, my breaths fast and shallow, because his damn finger has zeroed in on my g-spot. He strokes it relentlessly, driving me toward an inevitable climax. My belly tightens, as do my thighs, and we both know I'm close.

"I'm going to make you come so hard," he says, suddenly slipping down the bed, shoving the covers aside and settling between my legs. He pushes my thighs apart and wedges himself between them, his broad shoulders holding me open to his hungry gaze. He opens my folds gently, looking his fill as I start panting. My hands automatically go to his head, gripping his scalp with my short nails.

He groans as he lowers his mouth, flicking my clit with his hot tongue.

My hips heave up off the mattress. "Damn it, Jonah!"

He chuckles, but doesn't say anything. His mouth is far too busy for conversation. He licks and suckles my sensitized flesh. His long finger slips deep inside me, stroking my g-spot, while his tongue flutters powerfully against my clitoris. The onslaught of pleasure is overwhelming, and I come in a blinding explosion of pleasure, my nerves fried. My body shudders, and I swallow my cries, not wanting to advertise to our neighbors that we're having sex in the middle of the afternoon. These apartments aren't soundproofed.

"Fuck, Jonah!" I finally say, when I can speak again.

He licks me tenderly as I come down from my climax, residual tremors making me shake. When my body relaxes once more into the mattress, he rises up on his hands and knees and crawls up to me, his big body hovering over mine. He rests his hips between my thighs.

Leaning down, he kisses me, his lips damp and tasting like me, warm and salty. God, I love how he loves sex. I love how unabashed he is, how he revels in the act.

"I love you," he murmurs, his nose nuzzling mine. He kisses my forehead, and then the tip of my nose, before settling his mouth on mine once more. He coaxes my lips open and teases me with his tongue.

We kiss, long and languidly, and all the while he presses the hard ridge of his erection between my legs, coating his length in my body's slippery arousal. He teases my opening, pressing against me and retreating, driving me crazy until all I can think about is how badly I want him inside me. I'm aching with it. My hands clutch his hips, pulling him closer. "Jonah, please."

But he doesn't seem to be in any hurry. He rubs his length along my aching slit, teasing me, tormenting. This must be his way of getting back at me for my snarkiness. But two can play at this game. I reach between us and grasp his cock, positioning the head at my opening. Then I lift my hips, driving him a few inches inside me.

With a low growl, he sits back on his haunches and hooks his arms beneath my knees, raising my legs, opening me up even more.

His gaze is hot and hungry as he looks his fill.

"Why don't you just take a picture," I tell him, frustration edging my voice as I push against him. "Come on, pal. Fuck me already."

His heated glance reminds me that pay-backs are hell. Then he leans closer. His erection is so hard he has no trouble angling the tip at me and nudging the thick head inside my opening.

I gasp at the intrusion, and as he holds my legs wide and leans forward, pushing slowly inside me, I suck in a deep breath. Damn, he's a lot to take. I hope I never get used to it, because the feel of him pushing inside me is exquisite torture.

I'm already so aroused, soft and wet, that he's able to sink right into me, inch by inch, his thick shaft parting my flesh until he's fully seated, his heavy balls pressed against me.

Holding perfectly still, he blows out a long breath and grits his teeth. "Jesus."

I move against him, reveling in the way he fills me. It's so perfect, my heart stops and my breath catches. My body is still tingling head to toe from the mind-blowing orgasm he already gave me, and I swear to God I could come again.

When I move against him, feeling him slide along my nerve endings, he groans.

Now it's my turn to smile. He's on edge already, and he's fighting the urge to come. I start rocking my hips, and he releases my legs so he can come down onto me, pinning me to the mattress with all of his weight to hold me still. My breath leaves me in a whoosh. *Bastard!*

He links his fingers with mine and presses my hands into the pillow above my head. Then he looks into my eyes, communicating *everything*. "Not so fast," he murmurs, play-biting my jawline. "I'm nowhere near done with you."

When he starts moving, slowly at first, his jaw tightens and he tenses, grimacing at the pleasure. He closes his eyes as he sinks deep, all the way, and a muscle flexes in his cheek. Then his mouth descends on mine, hot and hungry, and he coaxes my lips open, slipping his tongue inside.

Our tongues play, frantically stroking and teasing, mimicking the movements of his cock inside me. In, out, stroking, teasing. I tighten my vagina, clamping down on his cock, wanting to milk his erection and drive him even higher.

He presses his forehead against my shoulder, letting out a harsh breath, followed by a groan. "God, Lia!"

His hips are moving faster now, with a growing sense of urgency. He releases my hands and sits back on his knees, his hands going to my knees as he pushes them wide. There's no hiding with Jonah. He stares down, mesmerized at the sight of his cock tunneling in and out of me. I raise my hips to meet each thrust, and he picks up his tempo, his jaws clenched as he drives in and out.

I clutch his thighs tightly, digging my nails into his muscles to egg him on. "More, Jonah! Harder!"

He's always so afraid of hurting me, but it's going to take more than a stiff fuck to do that. I *want* to feel his strength. With a growl, he lets himself go, powering in and out of me, pushing me higher up the bed with the force of his thrusts. His hands clamp down on my knees, and he holds me wide open. There's no hiding from his hot gaze, or his powerful thrusts. I can only grab the vertical bars of the headboard and hold on.

His neck muscles tighten, and he lifts his face to the ceiling, grimacing as he nears his climax. On and on, he powers into me, trying to draw this out as long as he can. I'm gasping and clutching his thighs, now, urging him on.

I love watching him come. I love seeing his body go rigid, the grimace on his face as his body explodes, the pleasure so great it almost hurts. I feel the force of his ejaculation hitting me deep inside, hot and molten. He presses his erection deep, and I feel him throb with each spurt. Eventually, he slows his movements as he gently slides through my slick channel.

"Jesus!" He releases my knees and comes down on top of me, still fully seated inside me. A moment later, he wraps me in his arms and rolls us to our sides so that he's not crushing me. "Fuck, tiger."

His nickname for me never fails to make me smile. It's a hell of a lot better than *sugar* or *baby* or something equally saccharine.

Breathing hard, he leans closer and presses his lips to mine. "I love you." Then he lifts my hand and kisses my ring finger.

I want to say the words back to him, but the lump in my throat is nearly choking me, making speech impossible at the moment.

He reads my gaze, a tender smile on his face. "It's okay. I know."

Jonah moves as if to pull out, but I clutch his arm. "No. Wait."

He stills, watching me as if he has all the time in the world.

Sometimes I hate the way I am. Even after years of therapy, I have trust issues. I have trouble allowing myself to be vulnerable with someone. But Jonah isn't Logan. Jonah would never betray me the way my first boyfriend did. "I love you."

He grins, looking ridiculously pleased at my admission. "That wasn't so hard, was it?"

I frown, because I know he deserves better from me. "Earlier, when you said we can't go on like this, and I thought you meant *us*, I... I was scared shitless, Jonah. I—you—I don't want to be without you. *Ever.*"

His expression softens, and he brushes my face gently. "You won't be, because I'm not going anywhere. I promise." He raises my hand and kisses my ring. "That's what this ring symbolizes—you and me together forever."

"I know I'm difficult," I say, stating the obvious and feeling the need to apologize for it. "I'm sorry."

He laughs. "You're not difficult. You keep me on my toes. There's a big difference." He presses my hand against his chest, right over his heart, and kisses me gently. "How about a quick shower before we go meet Jake and Annie?"

Honestly, I just want to lay here with him for a while longer. In quiet moments like this, I realize how lucky I am to have found him. After what Logan did to me, I honestly didn't think I could ever try again. But no, I'm not going there. I'm not going to ruin my post-coital bliss by dredging up my past. That's all behind me. I have Jonah now. And then I remember the way Jonah went after Logan, beating him black and blue. He busted the skin on more than a few of his own knuckles, right on Logan's smarmy face. The memory still makes me smile.

Jonah pats my naked hip as he gently pulls out. After he climbs over me and out of bed, he grabs my hand and hauls me to his side. "Shower."

"Wow, my third shower today," I say, following him into our bathroom. "This must be my lucky day."

# 4

## *Lia McIntyre*

By the time we're cleaned up and dressed, it's ten minutes before six. We leave our apartment and walk down the hallway to my brother Jake's apartment.

Jonah knocks, and Jake opens the door, standing tall as he practically fills the open doorway.

"Hey, man," my big brother says in his deep voice. He steps back for us to enter, offering me a fist bump. "Sis."

Jake and I knock knuckles, and then Jake shakes Jonah's hand. "Glad you two could make it. I hope you're hungry. We ordered Chinese. It should be here shortly."

"Starving," I say.

Jake shuts the door, and we three congregate in the living room.

I look around the room, half expecting to see Jake's girlfriend re-laxing on the sofa, with her feet up. She's been struggling with morn-ing sickness lately. "Where's Annie?"

Jake nods down the hallway. "Probably in our room, resting. She hasn't been feeling great lately."

*Morning sickness. Ugh.* Yet another reason why I think I'll leave the childbearing to the others.

Aiden, Annie's five-year-old son from a previous marriage, comes tearing down the hallway and practically careens into Jake. "Daddy! Can you open my yogurt, please?" The kid hands Jake one of those squishy yogurt drink pouches.

Jake tears off the top and hands the pouch back to him. "Here you go, pal. Where's your mama?"

Aiden makes a face. "She went back to bed. She said she's going to *puke.* Gross!" His big brown eyes widen when he turns his sights on us. "Hi, Aunt Lia! Hi, Uncle Jonah! Sorry, I can't talk right now. I'm *busy!*"

As the kid races back the way he came, I look up at my broth-er, who has a stupid grin on his face. I've never seen my brother so happy. "What the hell?" I say.

Jake shrugs. "There's no telling what that kid's up to." Then he loses his smile. "If you'll excuse me a minute, I want to check on Annie."

While Jake disappears down the hallway toward their bedroom, a security guard from the downstairs lobby announces through the intercom that our dinner has arrived.

"I'll go down and get the food," I say.

Jonah moves to follow me. "I'll come with you."

"No, *rock star*," I tell him, laying a restraining hand on his broad chest. "You wait here."

I head downstairs to collect our food order, leaving Jonah behind in the apartment. He hates being coddled, but it's for his own good. The security guards are good at keeping gawkers out of the front lobby, but every once in a while a few slip through, and Jonah gets mobbed.

I collect our sacks of food from the front desk, thanking the two guards on duty. Outside the glass doors, there's a small crowd of fans milling about the entrance, phone cameras at the ready, hoping for a Jonah sighting. A couple of them spot me and take some pics through the glass. Through my association with Jonah, I've become recognizable, which is the last thing I would wish for. I've had more than my fair share of fifteen minutes of fame, and I don't want to go through that again. Great, now I'll be all over Instagram and Snapchat today.

It's a shame people won't leave Jonah alone. The guy left L.A. partly because of the crowds, hoping to find anonymity in Chicago. Now, this apartment building is essentially a towering, gilded cage, keeping him trapped inside. We rarely go anywhere, other than to the recording studio, or occasionally to a local pub for an impromptu performance so he can practice his new songs. The poor guy rarely gets to go outside for fresh air and sunshine. Something's got to give.

When I return to the apartment, I rap on the door, and Jonah lets me in. Jake is carrying a laughing Annie down the hallway, relocating her from their bedroom to the living room. He lays her on the sofa and tucks her in with a blanket.

"Lia, hi!" Annie says, giving me a forced smile. She looks pale.

"I'm sorry you're not feeling well," I say as I set the sacks of food on the coffee table.

"Thanks, Lia," Jake says. Then he turns to Annie, opening the sacks and searching through the containers. "I ordered you some plain white rice." He picks up one of the cartons, opens it, and peers inside. "Here you go, baby." He hands her the container and a pair of chopsticks. "I also ordered you some plain steamed veggies, no sauce." He roots through the sacks for another container. "Hopefully this will help settle your stomach."

Who knew my brother could be such a bad ass partner? I have to give him props. He's taking really good care of his pregnant fiancée.

Jake catches me watching him and raises his dark slash of an eyebrow. "What?"

I shrug innocently. "Nothing."

Jake nods at the food cartons spread out across the coffee table. "You guys help yourselves. Dig in. I ordered plenty."

I grab some plates and serving utensils from the kitchen, and Jonah and I dish out some rice and entrees, beef and broccoli for him, sweet and sour chicken for me.

After Annie is settled with her plate and a bottle of water, Jake fills a small plate for Aiden, then a big, heaping plate for himself. He's got to eat a shitload of calories to maintain that two-hundred-eighty pound frame of solid muscle.

"Aiden!" Jake calls. "Come here, buddy!"

A moment later, Aiden comes tearing down the hallway into the living room, his green stuffed Stegosaurus tucked beneath his arm. "Yes, Daddy?" he says, breathless.

Jake sets Aiden's plate on the coffee table. "Sit here on the floor in front of your mama and eat your dinner."

Hearing Aiden call Jake *daddy* leaves a lump in my throat. The kid's biological father was an abusive asshole, and fortunately, he's no longer in the picture. I say *was* because the jerk's no longer breathing air. Jake took him out when Ted tried to shoot Annie practically point blank. My big hero brother threw himself between Ted and Annie, taking the bullet meant for her. Then he returned fire, ending Ted's reign of terror over Annie and Aiden.

When Jake and Annie—former high school sweethearts—reconnected after over a decade apart, Aiden wasted no time in adopting Jake as his new daddy. And of course Jake just eats it up. He's *so* ready for a family. And that's fortunate, since he accidently knocked Annie up within a few *days* of being reunited with her.

Jake and Annie are getting married in March, on their *special date*—the anniversary of their very first date eons ago, back in high school. Annie will be nine months pregnant by then. My family has a betting pool on whether she'll give birth *before* the wedding or *after*. I bet a hundred bucks that she'll pop ahead of her nuptials.

"Are you feeling any better?" I ask Annie after she's taken a couple of hesitant bites. I watch her pick cautiously at her food.

She gives me a tentative smile. "A little, yes. I usually feel better after I've eaten something. I don't want to miss our appointment to see the house this evening. I'm excited for you guys to see it. I think you'll like the neighborhood."

Jake and Annie have been looking for a house for a few weeks. With an active five-year-old, they want a kid-friendly environment for Aiden, so he can run outside and play.

Jonah and I have looked at a few houses on and off for a while now. Buying a house is serious business... like wearing engagement rings. I just couldn't bring myself to say yes. But then I think about how much better things would be for Jonah if we had a house with a modicum of privacy. He'd be able to go outside without being mobbed.

I look down at the ring he put on my finger. No one seems to have noticed it yet, or at least they haven't said anything about it. That's for the best. I certainly don't need to be razzed about wearing a stupid ring.

I find myself absently twisting the band on my finger, and then I notice Annie's gaze on me, a slight smile turning up the corners of her lips. Maybe I spoke too soon when I said no one had noticed.

I release the ring and wolf down my sweet and sour chicken. *Mmm.*

After we finish our meals—Annie barely touched hers, but at least she's feeling better—we get ready to head out. Jonah and I will ride with Jake and Annie in Jake's black Tahoe. There's a new gated community under construction in Lincoln Park, Jake tells us. There are twelve lots in all. Three houses have been built already on spec, and the rest of the lots are up for sale.

Jonah and I ride in the back seat with Aiden, who's seated in his booster chair. The kid's got Stevie, his Stegosaurus, perched on his lap so his dinosaur can see out the window.

Jake turns into the new subdivision, passing an empty guard station that's still under construction. "The community is fully gated," he says. "Twenty-four-seven guard presence at the gate. No one gets in without clearance. The entire subdivision is about twenty-six acres. Each lot is an acre, and then there are community spaces and green spaces. They're planning to put in a playground, a pond, and walking paths, and as you can see along the perimeter, there are plenty of trees for privacy."

A single, two-lane paved road leads into the development, with lots marked out on either side of the road. The road circles around at the far end, in a cul de sac formation. In the center of the cul de sac is a large, open green space.

"That's where the playground will go," Jake says. "It'll be fenced off to prevent kids from running into the street."

"Nice," I say, scanning the area as Jake pulls into the driveway of one of the three completed homes. A pair of two-story homes sit adjacent to each other on one side of the street. Directly across the street is a single story home.

Jake parks in the driveway of one of the larger houses, next to a black Mercedes coupe. "The sales manager is meeting us here," he says as he opens his door.

We pile out of the Tahoe and walk up the curving path to the front porch. A woman dressed in a cobalt blue, form-fitting skirt and jacket, perfectly poised on four-inch heels, greets us at the door, opening it and stepping back to let us in. Her ice-blonde hair is swept up in a graceful chignon.

"Welcome, Mr. McIntyre," she says, her voice silky smooth. She smiles first at Jake, then at the rest of us. "I'm so glad you could make it this evening."

"Can Stevie and I go upstairs to see our room?" Aiden asks, already heading for the curved staircase. It's obvious they've been here before, often enough for Aiden to feel right at home.

"Sure," Jake says. "Be good, and don't get lost."

"I won't get lost, Daddy," Aiden says, chuckling as he and his Stegosaurus climb the stairs.

The sales woman gives us a polished smile. "Make yourselves at home and have a look around," she says. And then she turns her smile on *me*. "Let me know if I can answer any questions, or if you'd like to see either of the other two houses. The one next door to this one is sold already, but the ranch home across the street is still available."

The saleswoman disappears into the dining room, which has been temporarily converted into a sales office. Jonah and I take in the sights as we follow Jake and Annie down the central hallway into the kitchen at the rear of the house.

There's a slick color brochure on the kitchen island. I pick it up and look at the floorplan of this house. Five bedrooms, four full baths. Two stories, plus a full finished walk-out basement. A three-car garage. A fitness room. A home theatre downstairs, and an office on the first floor.

*Five bedrooms? How many kids are they planning to have?* I lay the brochure down.

"Do you like it?" Annie says, giving me an encouraging smile. "I mean the community in general, not just this house."

I shrug. "Sure. What's not to like? It's private, protected, with lots of green spaces and trees. It's a great place for you guys to raise your kids."

Jake walks to the fancy stainless steel fridge and opens the door. "Want something to drink?" he says, looking at me and Jonah. "A beer? Soft drink? Water?"

"I'll take a beer," Jonah says.

"Same," I say.

Jake hands us our bottles of beer, and he hands a bottle of chilled water to Annie. He takes a Coke for himself. He seems awfully at home here, helping himself to the contents of the fridge.

Realization dawns. "You already bought this place, didn't you?" I say.

Annie blushes, and Jake nods. "We signed the papers yesterday," he says.

*Shit.* This is for real. My brother's all grown up now.

"The house across the street is available," Jake says, sounding far too casual for it to be just an idle comment. "Would you like to see it? We could be neighbors. How about that?"

A thought occurs to me, and I turn to Jonah. "Did you know about this?"

Jonah's expression transforms instantly, and he looks guilty as hell. "You did!" I say, dumbfounded.

*First the ring, and now we're looking at houses?* I'm starting to see a pattern here.

"Calm down, sis," Jake says, reaching out to brush the top of my head. "I might have mentioned to Jonah that Annie and I had decided to purchase a house in this community. I suggested to him that you guys check it out, too. I know you've been thinking about buying a house, and this community would be perfect. No more fan girls camping outside your door."

Jake pulls a keychain out of his front jeans pocket and tosses it to Jonah. "Go take a look." Then my brother eyes me directly. "There's no harm in looking, Lia."

I make a face at him, then turn and head to the front door, Jonah following me out. He snags my hand before I make it off the porch. "Slow down, tiger."

He holds my hand fast, and I can't easily pull away. My chest hurts, and a painful knot forms in my throat. I'm so fucking mad I could scream.

I turn to look at him, trying to compose myself. "My brother just *happened* to have a key to the house across the street in his pocket? Seriously? You two set me up."

"Lia." He pulls me to him, his hands cradling my face as he makes me look up at him. "We've been talking about buying a house for a long time—that's nothing new. This is a great community. Jake's family will be living here, too, right across the street. I thought you'd like that."

He's right—I would like that. But that's not the fucking point.

I love all my siblings, but I'm closest to Jake. He and I are a lot alike in some ways. For years, we've been there for each other. I helped him during his drinking years, and he helped me through my sex tape nightmare. I can't remember how many times we've called each other at three am for one crisis or another. We *get* each other, and we're there for each other. I can think of far worse things than living across the street from him. And Annie doesn't suck—in fact, I kind of like her. And her kid's hysterical.

For a moment, I lose myself in Jonah's dark eyes, taking comfort from them. He's my rock. The thought scares the hell out of me, because I don't know what I'd do if I lost him. He slides his arms around me, holding me steady, close. He's right. We have been talking for ages about buying a house, and the only thing stopping us is my damn cold feet. It's not fair to Jonah.

This location would be the perfect place to settle down. No crowds, no gawkers, no sobbing fans encroaching on his privacy. Hell, we'd even be able to sit out on the back porch and grill burgers like normal people. I know how much he'd like that.

He nods toward the house across the street. "Will you at least look at it? Please?"

My mind is racing, as is my pulse. This sure has been a day for surprises. "All right! I'll look at it."

He smiles, then lowers his mouth to mine. His lips are warm and coaxing, and he applies just the right amount of pressure. Just enough to make me go weak in the knees. *The bastard.*

# 5

## *Jonah Locke*

I take my recalcitrant girlfriend by the hand, holding it securely so she can't slip away from me, and lead her across the street. "We're just looking," I remind her, hoping to put her at ease.

I feel like I'm walking on eggshells here. Lia doesn't handle change well—that's one thing I've learned about her. She fears change, because she always assumes it will be for the worst.

We've talked about buying a house almost since we started dating. She supports the idea in theory, but when we get close to making a decision, she bolts.

I think she equates us buying a house with me putting an engagement ring on her finger. Maybe she sees it as a collar or a noose, and she rebels. Honestly, I'm not exactly sure. But I do know that she loves me. I never doubt that.

We walk hand-in-hand up the driveway to the house in front of us. It's definitely smaller than the other two houses, but still nice.

As we approach the front door, I squeeze her hand. "Remember, we're just looking."

It's an attractive house, with a brick and stone façade. The lawn is already nicely landscaped with young trees and shrubs and flower beds. There's a curved, brick path leading from the driveway to the front door.

"It has three bedrooms and three full baths," I tell her, having already committed the specs to memory. "And a two-car garage. There's a finished lower level with plenty of extra space."

We step up onto the front porch, and I take the key out of my pocket, unlocking the door. I push the arched, mahogany door open wide and motion for her to walk inside.

There's a sizable foyer with a crystal chandelier hanging high overhead form the vaulted ceiling. When I flip on the light, it casts an array of sparkling lights on the plain white walls and polished mahogany floors. Lia stands there, her expression perfectly neutral as she takes it all in. I have absolutely no idea what she's thinking.

I've known all along that my Lia is allergic to commitment. Her first boyfriend—back in high school—betrayed her in the worse way possible when she was just sixteen years old. Just thinking about that fucking sex tape makes me sick. What kind of asshole videotapes a sexual encounter with an underaged girl? A terrified virgin at that?

Logan Wintermeyer wasn't just a selfish prink; he was vindictive and cruel. He utterly humiliated a vulnerable young girl, broadcasting one of her most private and painful moments of her life for the public to view and ridicule. People can be such heartless assholes.

My chest tightens. My poor, damaged sweetheart.

"The walls are painted white," I say in a neutral voice, not wanting to pressure her. "We could choose our own paint colors, if we wanted something different."

Suddenly, she turns to me. "Have you already purchased this house?"

"No!" I say, surprised by her question. "I would *never* buy a house without your input and approval. I just said we'd *look* at it, that's all. We can walk away right now, if that's what you want."

She relaxes and resumes looking around.

There are rooms on either side of the entryway, one a home office, the other a sitting room with an entire wall of built-in bookcases and a fireplace. The central hallway leads past a powder room to the kitchen and a family room in the rear of the house. Beyond that, a pair of French doors leads to a solarium that overlooks a very private back yard.

I follow Lia into the kitchen, flipping on the lights as we go. The house is unfurnished, but it's far from cold. The cabinetry, fixtures, and wood floors are warm and inviting. Turning in a circle, she carefully takes everything in, stainless steel appliances, granite counters, and mahogany kitchen cabinets. "Fancy," she says.

"I guess so. Do you like it?"

She opens the fridge door and peers inside the empty appliance.

"The laundry room is through there," I say, pointing down a short hallway. "There's a pantry too. The bedrooms are down that hallway there. But there's something I want to show you first, downstairs. Something I think you'll like."

I take her hand and lead her down a carpeted staircase to the finished lower level. She follows reluctantly.

Downstairs there's a home theatre with a small kitchen, a full bathroom and a couple extra rooms that could be used as guest bedrooms. But I save the best for last.

I stop in front of an open doorway and flip on the lights inside an empty room. "This would make a great fitness room," I say. "There's plenty of room for all kinds of equipment. You could work out right here at home."

She studies the room, saying nothing.

I lead her further down the hallway, to a large room at the far end of the lower level. "And this room would make a great recording studio. I could have it soundproofed, so I could work and record in here without disturbing anyone in the house. I could work at *home*, Lia. Just think, you'd have your free time back to do whatever you wanted."

She pivots to look at me. "Is that what this is about? My *free* time?"

She looks...*hurt*. Shit! "You're with me twenty-four-seven," I tell her, trying to explain. "You have absolutely no time for yourself. We're either at our apartment, or we're at the recording studio. What kind of life is that for you?"

Her eyes narrow as she contemplates my words. "Jonah—"

"I don't want you to feel trapped, Lia... tied to me around the clock. If we lived here, I could compose and record from home. It would free up *hours* of your day so you could do whatever you want, go wherever you want. Since there's security on-site, you wouldn't have to babysit me every waking minute."

She frowns as she processes my words. "I don't need more *free* time, Jonah." She turns and heads back toward the stairs. She's quiet, lost in thought, and I think that's a good sign. If she were dead set against us buying this house, she'd come out and say so.

Once we're back in the kitchen, she turns to me. "It would cut down on your public visibility if we lived here. It would greatly reduce the risk of you being exposed out in the open, to the crowds, to the paparazzi. You wouldn't be so hemmed in all the time. You could go outside and do regular guy stuff."

Of course she would look at it that way—focusing on how this living situation would benefit *me*, or improve my privacy. But it's not *me* I'm worried about, it's *her*.

"This isn't common knowledge, yet," I say, "but you should know. Shane has purchased this entire community from the developers. It's going to be a private *family* development. He's already offered lots to your parents and to Beth's mom. I don't know about the rest of your siblings... Sophie or Hannah or Liam. And I don't know if Jamie and Molly are going to live here or not. They're undecided. But there's room enough for everyone who wants to live here."

Her eyes widen, and I can see her mentally putting all the puzzle pieces together.

"So, where would our bedroom be?" she says, abruptly changing the subject. "*Hypothetically.*"

"Hypothetically?" I can't help grinning, because she's actually considering this. She wouldn't be joking with me if she weren't halfway okay with the idea. "You want to see the master suite? It's got a sunken *hot tub* in the bathroom."

She shrugs, trying to act nonchalant, but I see a sparkle of interest in her clear blue eyes at the mention of the hot tub. "I might as well see it, since we're here."

I lead her down the hallway past two other bedrooms to the master suite, which is a large room with lots of windows, a vaulted ceiling, and a gas fireplace. There's also a huge walk-in closet, and a private bath. In addition to the hot tub, there's a walk-in shower big enough for a small crowd.

After inspecting the bathroom, she flips on the switch to the gas fireplace, igniting the flames. Then she walks to the windows overlooking the rear yard. About seventy yards out is a small forest. "It's certainly private," she says, as she absently twists the gold band on her finger.

"Yes, it is."

*A house and a ring, all on the same day.* I may be pushing my luck here.

But she surprises me when she walks up to me and grabs the waistband of my jeans, tugging me closer. "You want this? The house?"

I nod. "Yes. It will solve a lot of security issues for us. We'll have more freedom and privacy." *And, we'll have a house of our own.*

Her gaze searches mine, and I can see that her thoughts are racing. Then she shrugs, breaking the tension. "All right."

"All right? That's it?" I can't help the huge grin on my face as I pick her up and squeeze her. She laughs, and I kiss her soundly. "You won't regret this, I promise."

As I set her back down, her arms steal around my waist, and she presses up against me. Pulling my face down to hers, she kisses me. "This place feels good," she admits, sounding surprised. "We'll have space to breathe. We can spend time outside without watching over our shoulders constantly. We can cook outdoors, invite people over. Okay, let's do it."

Now it's my turn to kiss her. My hand cradles the back of her head, and slowly I back her up against the nearest wall, leaning into her, pinning her in place. She sighs, the tension easing from her body. Lia's always wound so tightly, always on guard and always hypervigilant. I've learned that sometimes she just needs to be able to let her guard down and feel safe. I can give her that.

I clutch both of her wrists in one hand and hold them above her head, pressed against the smooth surface of the wall. Then I trail kisses down her throat, suckling gently as I go. She shivers in my arms, melting as she relaxes.

"This house is going to be so good for us," I tell her, my lips pressed to her throat. I breathe in the scent of her warm skin, and instantly I start to harden.

"Can we make out in the hot tub?" she says.

I chuckle. "Yes. Any time you want."

Just as I cover her mouth with mine, someone rings the doorbell three times in rapid succession. A moment later, we hear the front door open, followed by Jake's deep voice and Aiden's giggle.

With a pained groan, I release her. "We have company."

She lets out a long breath. "No shit."

"Hey, where are you guys?" Jake calls, his voice echoing loudly through the empty house.

I can hear a woman's quieter voice—Annie? And then I hear the pitter patter of small feet—Aiden? I release Lia just as Aiden runs into the master suite.

"I found them, Daddy!" he yells. "They're in the bedroom!"

"Hey, Aiden," I say, stepping back and shifting my stance to accommodate my half-hard erection. I hope I don't sound as winded as I feel. "Yeah, you found us."

"Is this *your* bedroom?" he says, sounding awed as he notices the lit fireplace.

"It sure is," Lia says, ruffling the kid's short, spiky brown hair as she walks right past him and out of the room. "This is where the magic happens."

## 6

### *Jonah Locke*

re you sure?" I ask her that night as we're lying in bed. "If you want more time to think about it... or if you want to go back and look at the house again before making a decision, that's totally fine. There's no rush."

She stretches with a sigh. "No, I'm sure."

"Are you *really* sure? I didn't mean to pressure you into anything." I'm starting to get worried. She's taking this way too easily. Nothing's ever this easy with Lia.

"No, really, Jonah, it's fine. I love the house. We'll have our own secured family compound, just like the Kennedys. You'll have your own recording studio at home, and I can work out there as well. We'll be able to relax outside, take walks, cook out. It'll be great."

She slides her soft, supple thigh between mine, her skin deliciously cool. My dick begins to stir.

She makes an appreciative sound and turns to me, but the moment is interrupted when my phone buzzes with an incoming text message.

"I'm ignoring that," I say, pulling her closer.

My phone buzzes again, then again, in rapid succession. Someone's spamming me.

She sighs. "You might as well get it."

I grab my phone and check the screen. "Shit."

"Who is it?"

"Dwight."

"What the fuck?" She's silent for a moment, and then she lets out a heart-felt groan. "Please, not that asshat again. I can't take it."

I chuckle. Lia and my former manager, Dwight, did *not* get along when they first met, and that's putting it mildly. We haven't seen or heard from him since I left the label and he returned to L.A.

"What the hell does he want?" she asks.

I quickly skim his multiple messages. "He's here in Chicago for the weekend. He wants to meet with me tomorrow evening for a drink. And—oh."

"And what?"

"Never mind."

She grabs my phone and skims the conversation. "And... 'please don't bring your girlfriend.' Seriously?" She rolls her eyes. "What a fuckwad." Then she glares at me and says, "No."

"No?"

"You heard me."

I laugh. "Don't you want to know what he wants? Why he's here?"

"No." She tightens her arms around me and presses her belly against my groin. "Do you remember the shitstorm he caused the last time he was here?"

My phone chimes with another message from Dwight:

It's important, Jonah. We need to talk.

I kiss the top of her head. "He says it's important."

"No."

"Lia—"

"Okay, fine. But I'm coming with you. And I pick the venue. Tell him tomorrow night at Rowdy's, nine pm sharp. He gets thirty minutes with you, and not a second more."

I send Dwight the information. I am curious to hear what he has to say. My former band members have a new lead singer now, and the band has a new name. I want to know how they're doing... if they're happy. But if Dwight came here to talk me into returning to L.A. and to the recording label, he's wasting his time. I'm happy going it alone as a solo artist. In fact, I've never been happier than I am right now, both professionally and personally."

I pull Lia closer. Wanting to change the subject away from my former manager. "So, you're sure about the house?"

She slides her hand down to my dick, which is well on its way to becoming a full-blown erection. "Yes, I'm sure!" she says, clearly tired of me asking. "Now shut up and kiss me."

\* \* \*

Saturday morning, we sleep in after staying up half the night. I cook breakfast—eggs, bacon, and toast—and we eat in the living room, seated on the floor in front of the coffee table as we watch reruns of our favorite comedy show, *Key and Peele*.

After breakfast, Lia goes to our spare bedroom and runs on the treadmill while I camp out on the sofa to work on lyrics for the new song. She lifts weights while I put a load of laundry in the washer. She puts away the dried clothes while I work on the melody for my new song. This is how we roll... low key, just the two of us. We'd be fine stranded on a deserted island as long as we had each other.

Jake and Annie drop Aiden off at our apartment around noon while they run out for groceries. Aiden brings his stuffed dinosaur with him, as well as his favorite toy car.

The three of us eat peanut butter and jelly sandwiches for lunch and watch an animated dinosaur movie before Jake and Annie return to collect Aiden. I'm glad to see that Annie seems to be feeling better. They're both thrilled when Lia and I tell them we want the house.

As the afternoon progresses, Lia grows more and more antsy. Dwight is one of the last people she wants to see right now, or ever. I'm sure of it.

"Why don't you go beat the punching bag for a while?" I tell her. "Pretend it's Dwight. You'll feel so much better."

"Shut up, Jonah."

* * *

At eight-thirty, Lia and I head down to the garage and set off in the Jeep for Rowdy's. The pub is located in Old Towne, not too far from our apartment. Lia finds a parking spot on the street just two blocks from the pub, and we walk. I'm wearing a baseball cap in an effort to conceal my hair, as well as a pair of fake black-rimmed eye glasses. It's too late in the evening for sunglasses—that would call even more attention to me. My goal is to be invisible. Anonymous. Sneak in without garnering too much attention, then sneak out just as quietly.

Rowdy's manager—Ron Stanley—is a friend of Shane's. We called ahead and reserved a table in the back corner, pretty much out of sight of onlookers. They don't normally take reservations, but thanks to Ron's friendship with Shane, we get special treatment.

Rowdy's is packed tonight, as is typical for a Saturday night. It's a popular spot for locals—both blue collar and white. A lot of folks come here to watch sports on the big flat screen TVs positioned all around the dining room. And the food's good.

We walk in the front doors, and we're greeted immediately by a female server, Crystal, who's expecting us. She walks us to our table in a private corner, behind a folding screen and some plastic potted plants.

Our server is probably in her thirties, with a strong punk vibe. She wears her black hair shaved on one side, longer on the other, and she sports a number of visible tattoos on her arms and an array of facial piercings. She looks me over once, more out of curiosity than anything. "Can I get you guys something to drink?"

"I'll have a Coke," Lia says. Then she points at me. "He'll have a draft beer."

Technically, Lia's on duty right now, so she won't touch alcohol. I, on the other hand, can drink. Not only do I have a personal bodyguard, but I have my own designated driver. I never drink to excess, but one or two beers won't hurt me as long as I'm eating too.

"We'll take an order of hot wings and onion rings," I say.

Our drinks come, and then our food. Nine o'clock comes and goes with no sign of Dwight. That's a little surprising, as he's normally quite punctual. He's the one who loves to complain when others are late.

Lia and I are halfway through our drinks and appetizers when Crystal escorts Dwight to our table.

He's a thin man, of medium-height with a narrow face and a cagey expression. His light brown hair is thinning, and he styles it in an attempt to conceal the fact that he's going bald.

Dwight catches sight of Lia sitting with me and his step falters for a moment, a frown marring his brow. Subtlety is not one of his finer points.

"Sorry I'm late!" Dwight says sounding winded as he slides into the chair opposite mine. He reaches across the table for a handshake. "It's great to see you again, Jonah! You're looking well."

I shake his hand, waiting for him to acknowledge Lia's presence. Finally, he tosses her a glance, clearly an afterthought. "Hello, Lia."

I'm annoyed by how dismissive he is of my girlfriend. If I thought she cared one iota, I'd be offended on her behalf and take issue with

Dwight. But, honestly, she doesn't care. Not one bit.

Lia picks up her glass and glares at Dwight, making absolutely no apologies. "You're half an hour late," she says. "I was beginning to hope you wouldn't show."

Lia's tone is so derisive, I have to bite my lip to keep from grinning. Leave it to my better half to put assholes in their places.

"So, Dwight," I say, as he stares distractedly at his phone screen. "What brings you back to Chicago?" My goal is to get this conversation moving. The sooner he tells me why he came, the sooner I can say *no*, and the sooner we can go home. There's absolutely nothing Dwight could offer that I'd be interested in.

He glances once more at his phone before setting it down close by. Then he looks at me. "I've talked to the label execs on your behalf, and they're willing to offer you a premium package if you'll come back."

Dwight eyes me expectantly, as if he expects me to get up and do cartwheels.

I shake my head. "I've told you before, Dwight. I'm not interested in coming back. I'm quite happy with the way things are."

Dwight makes a scoffing sound, making it clear what he thinks about my status as an indie artist. His phone starts chiming a string of notifications, and he glances once more at the screen.

Crystal returns to the table to take Dwight's drink order, and he opts for a rum and Coke.

"Have you actually looked at the Top Twenty chart lately?" Lia asks Dwight as she reaches for a boneless chicken wing. She pops it into her mouth and talks as she chews. "Jonah's kicking ass on his own. He doesn't need a record label or a manager, for that matter."

Dwight scowls at her, and then he turns his attention back to me. "They're willing to offer you one mil more than your previous contract. They're serious, Jonah."

"So am I," I say, reaching for my beer and taking a swig. "I'm not interested. If you came all this way just to ask me that, you could have saved yourself a lot of time and just called."

Lia's phone chimes with an incoming notification, and she glances at her phone and frowns. Two more chimes arrive on the heels of the first one. A moment later, Crystal walks up behind Lia and whispers in her ear.

Lia looks up at the young woman, saying nothing, but I can tell from the sudden tension in her frame that there's a problem.

"What is it?" I ask her.

Instead of answering me, she pivots to Dwight. "You idiot! You fucking broadcasted his location."

Dwight's lips flatten, and he returns her icy glare. "Jonah needs to see what *I* bring to the table, and that's *publicity*."

Lia stands, glancing hard at me. She has clearly shifted into security mode, and when she's in security mode, she means business. "I'll be right back," she tells me, her voice tight. "Don't you dare leave this spot." And then she stalks off, her pace brisk and determined.

"What did you do?" I ask Dwight, although I'm pretty sure I can guess.

He helps himself to an onion ring. "I didn't do anything."

I raise a brow at him, not believing for a second.

He shrugs as he checks his phone. "I may have posted on social media that we were meeting here this evening. I'm sure there's a sizable crowd outside this establishment right now. That's what I can bring to you. Besides the backing of the label and a guaranteed income, I can provide you with *publicity*. Tons of it."

The idiot knows absolutely nothing about me if he thinks that's an effective selling point. The very *last* thing I want is publicity.

I stand, pulling out my wallet and grabbing two twenties to lay on the table. "As soon as Lia returns, we're leaving."

Dwight straightens in his seat. "What! You can't leave! We're just getting started."

"Oh, no. We're done."

$\wp$ 7

## Lia McIntyre

I'm so fucking livid I could rip that bastard's head clean off his shoulders. Dwight fucked us over. He announced on all the top social media platforms that Jonah would be here tonight, and the news is spreading like wildfire.

I stalk to the front of the pub, where Ron and his bouncer, a massive muscle guy named Tim, are standing in front of the glass doors.

"I had to lock the doors," Ron says when I join them. An older guy with buzzed white hair and a salt-and-pepper beard, Ron Stanley is former military, which puts me somewhat at ease. He knows how to handle situations, and he knows the damage an unchecked crowd can do.

The sidewalk outside Rowdy's is filled with people standing shoulder to shoulder, pushing and crowding the entrance. There are plenty of fan girls here, but also paparazzi, their cameras shooting everything that moves. Even the local news outlets have reporters and camera crews here, too. *Fuck.*

"I estimate there are close to two hundred people out there," Ron says. "And the crowd is growing by the minute. You guys need to evacuate the premises immediately."

I nod.

Crystal runs up to join us, breathless. "There's a crowd out back, too," she says. "In the alley. Nowhere near as big as this one, but I'd say at least fifty people."

*Shit.*

There are customers wanting to leave the pub, but they're stuck inside at the moment because Ron doesn't dare unlock the doors with that crowd out front. There are also people—actual customers—wanting to come inside the pub, but again, same problem.

"I'll have to call for back-up," I say to Ron as I grab my phone.

He nods, his expression grim. "I'm sorry, Lia. It's just me and Tim here tonight, and if we open these doors, I don't think we can hold this crowd back on our own."

After making a call to Jake, I head back to our table to collect Jonah.

He sees me coming, and he's clearly irritated by the mess Dwight has created. "Let's get out of here," he says.

I shake my head. "It's too late. There are at least two hundred people out front, and another fifty at the rear door. We're penned in and outnumbered."

I reach for my gun, which is sitting in the holster at my lower back, and pop out the magazine to check the rounds. I snap the magazine back in, maybe a little harder than necessary.

Dwight looks a little green around the gills. "I'll go talk to them."

I roll my eyes at Dwight as I holster my gun. "No thanks, asshat. You're the reason we're in this mess. I'm sure as hell not going to let you go out there and fucking *confirm* that Jonah's here." I turn my back on Dwight. "I called Jake for back-up," I tell Jonah. "Their ETA is ten minutes."

Then I turn back to Dwight. "If you say one fucking word about Jonah, or even touch your God-damned phone, I will break every one of your fingers. Do you understand me?"

"You can't do that," he says, making a sour face.

I grin, hoping like hell he'll test me. "Just try me, asshole. Please! I dare you."

Jonah shakes his head at Dwight. "I'd believe her if I were you."

My phone chimes with another message, and I check the screen. "That's our cue," I tell Jonah. "Time to go." And then we walk away from Dwight without another word. I'm itching to give him a whipping, but right now my focus is on getting Jonah safely out of here. I couldn't care less about what happens to Dwight.

We head down the hallway to the door that leads into the rear alley. Ron's waiting for us, standing just a couple of feet from the door, watching out a small window.

I join Ron and peer out the smudged panes of glass at the narrow space behind the building. The alley is jam-packed with bodies, and it's not just fans out there. There are plenty of paparazzi too.

"Killian and Cameron will create a diversion in front of the pub," I tell Jonah. "Jake and Charlie will pick us up here."

I hate this. The alley is dark and cramped, and there are a shit-load of people out here. I hate putting Jonah at risk like this. The situation is unpredictable, and he could get hurt. Sure most of these gawkers are harmless, but you never know when a loose cannon is going to show up. If anyone's going to get hurt, it won't be Jonah. I'll make damn sure of it.

Ron's watching out the window, waiting to signal us when the Tahoe is in position.

"They're here!" Ron calls. "Go!"

I unlock the metal door and push it open a few inches to confirm. Jake's black Tahoe is parked right in front of the door, as close as it can be and still give us room to open the door. Charlie's behind the wheel, and Jake's out of the vehicle already, his brawny arms creating a barricade as he pushes the crowd back. "Move it, folks!" he bellows, his deep voice ricocheting like thunder in the crowded alley.

He opens the Tahoe's rear passenger door. "Get in!" he tells us.

Jonah makes a dash for the SUV, and I follow right behind him, climbing in after him and closing the rear passenger door. As soon as we're in the clear, Jake hops into the front passenger seat, closes the door and engages the locks.

Charlie puts the vehicle in gear and slowly heads to the main road. "Having fun, kids?" she says, grinning at us in the rearview mirror.

"Hardly," I say, finally relaxing as I buckle my seat belt.

Jake turns in his seat. "What happened?"

"Jonah's former manager is what happened," I say. "That asshat announced on social media that Jonah was meeting him here for drinks tonight. He caused this shitstorm—intentionally."

"I take it you don't like this guy," Charlie says as she pulls out onto the main road.

"That's putting it mildly. Hey, thanks for coming out tonight, guys. We appreciate it."

Charlie smiles. "No problem. Happy to help."

"Speaking of vehicles," Jake says, "where's your Jeep?"

I gesture down the street. "It's parked two blocks north of Rowdy's."

Charlie drives us to the Jeep, and Jonah and I transfer vehicles, thanking our back-up crew again. "Tell Killian and Cameron thanks, too," I tell them.

Charlie nods. "Will do. Call us anytime."

Jonah's awfully quiet on the drive back to our apartment building, staring out the passenger window.

"Hello? Earth to Jonah."

He shakes himself out of his reverie and looks at me. "Sorry, what?"

"Is everything okay? You looked like you were a million miles away just now."

He frowns. "It was a mistake to agree to meet with Dwight. I'm sorry."

"Oh, hell, it's not your fault. Dwight's an idiot."

He smiles reluctantly. "Someone could have gotten hurt tonight."

And of course by *someone*, he means *me*. He never worries for himself. "Again, it's not the rock star's fault."

His smile broadens. I think he likes it when I call him that.

After parking in the underground lot, I turn off the engine and relax back into the driver's seat. Mission accomplished. We're home, safe and sound.

As we exit the vehicle, I do a quick scan of the area for any threats. There are two young women watching us from about twenty yards away, their eyes on Jonah. They seem harmless enough as they stand chatting quietly beside a little blue Miata. The blonde blushes, but the brunette gives Jonah a blatant, come-hither stare.

Just about everyone who lives in our building knows he lives here—you'd have to be living under a rock not to have heard. And overall, they're pretty good about respecting his privacy. I don't mind if they stare at him, as long as they keep their distance and don't crowd him or touch.

"Want to watch a movie tonight?" Jonah asks as we ride up in the elevator. He throws his arm across my shoulders and pulls me to stand in front of him. He wraps his arms around me, and a moment later, I feel his lips in my hair. I shiver.

"A movie sounds good." I lean back against him, his broad chest at my back a comfort, as are his arms wrapped securely around me.

He rests his chin on the top of my head. "Just you, me, a couple beers, and the sofa," he says wistfully, his hand sliding beneath the hem of my sweatshirt to stroke my bare skin, electrifying me.

My body responds instantly to his touch, as heat pools between my legs. I clench my vagina, which feels achingly empty right now. It wants to be filled. By him. Honestly, the last thing I want to do right now is watch a movie. I can think of something I'd much rather be doing. But he wants to watch a movie, so I'll go along with it.

His hand slides up my torso, his fingertips grazing the side of my breast. Somehow, I think we're on the same page.

## 8

*Lia McIntyre*

Jonah changes into a pair of flannel drawstring pants, which ride low on his lean hips, and nothing else. The sight of his bare chest and arms, decorated with striking black ink makes my ache worse, and I just want to lick his tattoos. I'm not sure if he consciously set out to tease me, or if he just doesn't realize how fucking sexy he is.

I freshen up in the bathroom, then pull on a pair of loose knit shorts and a tank top—*no panties*. I'm getting lucky tonight.

When I join him in the living room, he's got two cold beers— Zombie Dust, my favorite—sitting on coasters on the coffee table.

"It's your turn to pick," he says, handing me the remote control. While I'm scanning our watchlist on Netflix, calling out movie titles for him to consider, he systematically turns off *all* the lights in the apartment and opens the drapes behind the sofa fully, exposing our front-row view of downtown Chicago and Lake Michigan. It's a clear, cloudless night, and the stars flicker brightly overhead. The city's night skyline is lit up like a Christmas tree with twinkling lights.

Jonah's definitely up to something. I can tell.

I select a new action film, one with lots of car chases and gunfights, and have it cued up to start when he joins me on the sofa.

"Oh, good," he says, liking my choice of movie. "We've been wanting to see that one."

"Is there a reason why you turned off every single light in the apartment?" I ask him, unable to hide my grin.

He shrugs, his eyes glued to the opening credits on the flat screen TV. "Nope."

*Liar.*

As the movie starts, Jonah lays his hand on my bare leg, patting it a couple of times before sliding his warm fingers between my thighs. Seems innocent enough.

He hands me an ice cold bottle of Zombie Dust, and I take a swig as he takes a drink of his own.

The movie starts, but I'm finding it hard to concentrate because he's using the tip of his finger to draw lazy little circles on my inner thigh. He knows how crazy it makes me when he touches me *there*. If he wanted to have sex, he could have just said so. I don't get why we're going through the motions of *pretending* to watch a movie.

We're ten minutes into the movie and I couldn't tell a thing that's happened, other than there's been a lot of gunfire and a few car chases. It looks like someone's trying to rob a high-security bank. My eyes might be directed at the screen, but my attention is glued to the way his blunt fingertip moves languidly across my skin. It's hypnotic.

I wait patiently for him to make his move. When he does, he surprises me. His hand slips out from between my thighs, and he lifts my left hand to his mouth. He kisses my ring finger, his lips warm on my skin. *It's only a placeholder ring? Yeah, sure it is.*

His finger returns to what it was doing a moment ago—drawing lazy circles on the sensitive skin between my thighs, just inches from my crotch. *Seriously?* Who does he think he's kidding?

I'm practically holding my breath in anticipation, waiting for that finger to slide inside my shorts. I know it's going to—it's only a matter of time. When it finally slides beneath the fabric and grazes the lips of my sex, my body tightens with need. A sound escapes me, something awfully close to a whimper, and I press my head against the back of the sofa and close my eyes. Fuck the movie.

His fingertip slides between my folds, skimming along my slit and collecting wetness, which is pooling at an alarming rate. Once his finger is coated, he seeks out my clit, gently brushing the hypersensitized little bit of flesh.

The movie plays on, but without sound. It takes me a moment to realize that he must have hit the mute button. There's a crazy shoot out on the screen, but the only sound I hear is my own heavy breathing... and his.

I squirm as his slick finger torments me. "Jonah?"

"Hmm?"

"What are you doing?"

"Isn't it obvious?"

His wet finger slides downward and dips inside me. I let out a harsh groan and widen my legs to give him room. "Jonah!" My breathy voice is tinged with impatience and frustration.

I glance down at his lap, and even in the dark I can see the thick ridge of his erection pressing against his PJ bottoms. Hungry for a closer touch, I climb onto his lap, sitting astride and facing him. I lower myself onto him, straddling his cock, and groan at the firm heat pressed against me. The thin fabric between us does little to separate our bodies.

Riding him like a cowgirl, I grind myself against him on the sofa. The vista stretching out in front of me, beyond the windows, is the Chicago night skyline. It's a fucking turn on, making out in front of a window under the cover of darkness—but I suspect he already knew I'd feel that way. No one can actually see what we're doing, but the feeling of discovery is tantalizing. It feels wicked and naughty and hot as hell, all at the same time.

Shamelessly, I move on him, rolling my hips against his rigid length. The wet heat of my sex sinks through the fabric, further fueling his erection. I'm aching now, desperate for more. More friction, more pressure. Wanting him to fill me.

His hands clamp down on my hips, and he urges me on. His mouth finds mine, eating hungrily at me, both of us breathing hard.

A long, drawn-out whimper escapes me, and he smiles against

my lips. *The bastard.* He knows exactly what he's doing to me.

Well, two can play at this game. I pull off my tank top and toss it on the sofa, freeing my breasts, creating a distraction he can't resist. His gaze goes right to my tits, and while he's staring at them, I shimmy out of my shorts and toss them aside too, leaving myself buck naked.

As I rock against him, his hands clamp on my waist, his fingers flexing strongly. I cup a breast, holding its warm, heavy weight in the palm of my hand. The nipple appears a deep plum color in the dark, and I tease it with my index finger, making it tighten into a pebble. I'm not above using my assets to gain the upper hand.

Jonah swallows hard, his gaze glued to my breast. I smile when his tongue comes out to lick his lip. *Men.* They're so predictable. "You see something you like?" I murmur.

His nostrils flare hotly and his eyes narrow. "Jesus, Lia."

I smile. "I'll take that as a *yes.*"

I release my breast and clasp my hands on his shoulders. Then I get serious about rocking myself on him, using the thick ridge of his erection to drive up my own arousal. I rock, hard and deep on him, until we're both sucking in air.

He reaches for the waistband of his bottoms and lifts his hips, raising me with him as he shoves his pants down far enough to expose his cock.

When I sink back down on him, there's nothing between us. It's just my wet, hot flesh rubbing against his equally hot, thick erection. The friction is mind-blowingly sweet.

"God, Lia!" he grinds out between clenched jaws as his fingers flex on my hips.

I study his face, at the muscle flexing in his jaw. His eyes are glittering with arousal, dark and intense, his muscles drawn tight. Everything about him is taut and on edge.

God, he's gorgeous when he's aroused.

I smile as I rub my clit against the thick base of his cock, feeling the coarse hairs brush against my sensitive flesh, teasing me taunting me. His hands grasp my hips, clenching tightly, hard enough to leave bruises, but I don't care. I'm about two seconds away from coming, and the anticipation is so delicious I could die happy right now.

I lean forward and brush my lips against his, lightly, teasingly. "You feel so fucking good," I say. Then I lick his bottom lip. My breath is shallow and shaky, and I'm about to fly apart any second. "I'm *so* close, Jonah. *So close.*"

"Wait," he growls, reaching frantically between my thighs. He grips his erection and lifts it, angling it toward my opening. "Put me inside you, quick! I want to feel you come."

The sound of his voice—urgent and rough—ratchets up my arousal even higher. Seeing him turned on turns me on. I reach down and fist the base of his cock, positioning the thick crown at my opening. Letting out a sigh, I sink down on him, gasping when the broad head of him breeches my opening and lodges inside. His hands return to my hips, and he holds me in place as he raises his hips, driving himself deeper inside me, rocking in and out, sinking further each time.

The feeling of fullness is exquisite, and I gasp.

"That's it, baby," he croons with a harsh groan. "Let me in."

He bucks his hips, driving deeper. I let out a breath, forcing my body to relax and let him inside. Once he's fully seated, he holds me still, my body impaled on his. He rocks his hips slowly. I start moving again, chasing my orgasm, which is still hovering close. His hands slide behind me to cup my ass as I rock on him, riding him shamelessly.

When my climax is imminent, I lean forward and kiss him, coaxing his lips open and teasing his tongue with mine. As our tongues tangle, his hands come around to cup my breasts, squeezing and shaping them. He gently pinches my nipples, sending a shudder coursing through me. I tense, arching my back as my body detonates. My nerves sing as pleasure sweeps through me, wave after wave, drawing out a hoarse cry.

As my climax begins to wane, I clamp down on his cock, squeezing him tightly. His hands cup my ass cheeks, and he holds me to him as he thrusts hard, grunting loudly as he works himself inside me. He bucks, harder and faster as his hips work like a piston, shoving himself into me, pulling back.

"Fuck!" he shouts, his voice raw. His mouth locks on mine and he gasps as his body erupts inside me. He shoves deep, holding himself there as his cock throbs. I can feel the heat of his ejaculation searing my insides, wave after wave.

"Jesus, Lia," he groans, leaning his forehead against mine. His chest heaves as he tries to catch his breath. "God, baby!"

He dips his mouth down to mine, kissing me with shaking lips.

Jonah's arms go around me, and he holds me tightly to his chest.

I can feel his heart hammering. I know mine is.

He works his PJ bottoms off his legs, then stands with me still joined to him. He carries me down the hallway to our bedroom, straight into the bathroom to clean up.

We end up in bed soon after, both of us feeling boneless and satiated. He pulls the bedding over us, and we lie entwined.

"You're going to be the death of me," he murmurs, pressing his lips to my forehead.

I chuckle, thinking I could say the same thing. "Yeah, but it's a great way to go."

He laughs, rolling onto me. "Yes. It is."

Jonah links our hands and holds them firmly on the pillow, above my head. The feeling of being restrained like this is both a curse and a turn on. I hate feeling overpowered, immobilized, and yet the weight of him on me is comforting. He slides a thigh between mine, further trapping me beneath him.

I make a sound, part protest and part... submission? Jesus, where did that come from? He smiles. When I make a half-assed attempt to break free of his hold, he tightens his grip and lets his weight settle more firmly on me.

I buck beneath him. "Let me up."

But he doesn't. If anything, he doubles down. I don't know what he's up to, but obviously he's trying to make a point.

He looms over me, his eyes locked on mine. "Do you trust me?" His voice is low, steady.

I shrug, feeling increasingly uneasy. I don't know where this is going, and it's making me nervous. We just had mind-blowing sex, and now he's ruining it by getting all serious on me. I buck into him, half-heartedly trying to dislodge him, but he doesn't budge. I grit my teeth. *Do I trust him?* "Don't be an idiot."

He grins. "I'll take that as a *yes.*"

"Yeah? So what?" My heart starts pounding, but not in a good way. "What the fuck are you doing, Jonah? Get off me."

He shakes his head. "We need to talk."

"Oh, hell no! Don't ruin my sex high." I try to pull my hands free, but he tightens his grip.

"Do you love me?" he asks calmly, as if I'm not trying to escape his hold.

When I buck against him, he slides his thigh deeper between mine, his wiry hairs brushing against my tender skin. He presses his thigh against my pussy, which is still throbbing and damp.

"Lia, do you love me? It's not a difficult question."

I make a face, wishing he'd stop this—whatever it is he's doing. But he keeps watching me, waiting for an answer, and I have a feeling he's not going to let up unless I give him one. "Yes. You know I do."

He nods, making it clear he expected as much. "Then why do you freak out on me every time I try to put a ring on your finger? Is it so difficult for you to imagine us as husband and wife?"

# 9

## *Lia McIntyre*

I do not freak out every time you try to put a ring on my finger!"

"Yes, you do! Are you not sure of me? Is that it? Are you not sure of *us*?"

He actually sounds hurt, as if that could even be a possibility. "Yes, I'm sure of you. Of us."

"Then why won't you even contemplate marrying me? We've been together for nearly two years, Lia. That's not an insignificant amount of time."

I swallow hard, past the lump forming in my throat. I feel tears pricking the back of my eyes, but I refuse to cry. "I didn't know there was a deadline."

"Of course there's not a deadline. But I'm not getting any younger, and I know what I want. Who I want. And that's you. What's holding you back? What are you afraid of?"

I really don't want to talk about this because it leads to nowhere good. I buck against him. "Enough, Jonah. Let me up."

Despite the edge in my voice, he shakes his head. "No. Not until you explain what you're feeling."

When I think about all the women I know—Beth, Molly, Erin, my sisters Hannah and Sophie, my mom—I always come up short in comparison. They're all well educated. They all have interesting careers. They all have a sense of direction and purpose. What do I have? My interests are martial arts and target practice. I love kicking ass and shooting things. I love action movies. I'm impulsive and a regular pain in the ass... just ask my brothers. What can I possibly offer Jonah, other than physical safety and security?

"Are you afraid you'll grow tired of me?" he says. He means it as a joke, but I detect an underlying vulnerability.

I laugh. "No. I'm afraid *you'll* grow tired of *me*." There! I said it.

He frowns. "What in the hell are you talking about?"

"You could have anyone, Jonah. All kinds of intelligent, fascinating women would jump at the chance to be with you. What can I offer you? Nothing."

He looks dumbfounded, almost angry. "Are you serious?"

Now he's just pissing me off. "I've had enough. Get off me!"

His hands tighten on mine. "No. Back in L.A., I dated a lot of women. Pop stars, actresses, lawyers, doctors, teachers, CEOs, musicians. I even dated an astrophysicist once, and a ballerina. Hell, I can't even remember all the women I dated. They threw themselves at me. But *none* of them ever made my heart pound when she walked in the room. None of them made my hands shake or my palms sweat. I never craved their attention or hung on their every snarky word. None of them ever made me feel like I feel when I'm with you. I can't quantify what I feel for you, Lia. I can't define it. All I know is I want to be part of your life. I don't want to live without you—*ever*."

Tears well up and spill over my lashes, trailing down the sides of my face. His expression softens as he releases my hands so he can grab the box of tissues on my nightstand. He pulls out a tissue and gently dabs at the wetness on my cheeks. "I don't have the slightest doubt about you or us, Lia. This is it for me. You're it. Have I not made that clear?"

I take the tissue from him and wipe my eyes, giving myself a moment to process. It can't be this easy—it just can't. "We haven't even talked about kids, Jonah. Honestly, I'm not sure I even want them. I'd be a shitty mom."

Jonah laughs. "No, you wouldn't. But kids aside, all I care about is having you in my life—forever. The rest is just details we can work out as we go. If you want kids, fine. If you don't, that's fine too."

He's being so honest, putting himself out there. The least I can do is meet him halfway. "I *am* afraid you'll grow tired of me," I say, my throat tightening around a knot. "I'm so afraid you'll wake up one day and realize that."

He grabs my left hand and brings it up so that we're both looking at the gold band he placed on my finger. My *placeholder* ring. I have a feeling he sees it as much more than a placeholder.

"Please marry me, Lia. Please trust me and take a chance on me. I promise, I won't let you down."

My stupid tears keep coming, and Jonah hands me a fresh tissue.

I press the tissue to my cheeks, soaking up the hot tears. "Okay, fine!" I say, choking on the words. "But don't blame me if you wake up one of these days and realize you've made a terrible mistake."

He grins, his own eyes glittering with tears. "Is that a *yes*?"

I shrug. "I guess so."

He grips my chin gently. "You have to *say* it, tiger. Say '*Yes, I will marry you, Jonah.*'"

I roll my eyes. "You are such a drama queen. Okay! *Yes, I will marry you, Jonah.* Are you happy now?"

"Very." He rolls onto his back, his arm draped over his forehead. "I'm in shock. She said yes."

I wave a hand dismissively. I'm done making big decisions for one night. "Fine. Whatever."

He laughs as he rolls up over me once more, sliding his thigh between mine, nudging them open enough that he can nestle his hips between my legs. His hand goes to my breast, gently kneading the flesh before dipping down to kiss my nipple reverently.

A wave of pleasure rolls through me, settling deep in my belly. He wants to marry me, even after I reminded him of all the reasons why he shouldn't. He's still willing to take that chance. *On me.* I guess the least I can do is take a chance, too.

His lips travel up past my shoulder, up my neck, to the soft spot beneath my ear, the one that makes me shiver. When his lips are against my ear, he whispers, "I promise you won't regret this."

"What's my favorite movie?" I ask him.

"Deadpool," he answers immediately.

"My favorite food?"

"Chinese."

"My favorite band, not counting you?"

He chuckles. "Seether."

"My favorite beer?"

"Zombie Dust."

"I guess you have been paying attention, rock star."

He nips my earlobe, making me squeal. "You better believe I have." He leans forward to kiss me. "I love you, Lia."

To my utter shock, I feel my cheeks heat. I never blush! "I love you, too."

He grins, looking utterly pleased with himself. "Now that wasn't so hard, was it?"

# ౿ 10

## *Lia McIntyre*

I awake Sunday morning before Jonah does. We're still wrapped in each other's arms from a late night of lovemaking. I still can't believe we're engaged. It's not that I don't love him, or I'm not sure. I'm absolutely sure of him. I'm just not convinced he won't wake up one day and regret tying himself to me.

I lift my left hand and stare at the gold band. Just looking at it makes my pulse kick up. There's no going back now, not that I want to.

My watch chimes, reminding me to take my birth control pill. I disentangle myself from Jonah's arms and reach into the top drawer of my nightstand for the little white pack of pills and pop one out, swallowing it with a swig of water from the bottle I keep beside my bed. I am meticulous about taking my pill at the exact same time every day. No mistakes. No unplanned pregnancies... not for me. Unplanned pregnancies seem to run in my family... both Beth and Annie got knocked up unintentionally. Of course they were both ecstatic about it, both eager to be moms, but still. It just happened. No thanks!

I climb quietly out of bed, so as not to wake Jonah, and hit the bathroom before heading to the kitchen. All that drama last night makes me hungry this morning. I pop a bagel in the toaster and get out the blueberry cream cheese.

Sitting at the breakfast counter, I'm nibbling my bagel and drinking my first cup of coffee for the morning when my phone chimes with an incoming text message from Beth:

**Got plans for lunch? Come up and join us? We have news.**

*News?* She and Shane probably want to tell us about the gated community Shane has commandeered.

I send her a reply:

**Sure. I've got some news of my own.**

She replies:

**What news? OMG, what's up?**

I chuckle as I send a reply:

**Relax. It's nothing Earth shattering.**

Jonah strolls into the kitchen just as I'm finishing my first cup of coffee. He's got his drawstring PJ bottoms on, riding low on his hips.

I can see his lean hip bones and the sexy trail of dark hair that arrows down to his penis. *Damn.* If marrying him means I get to look at this every morning for the rest of my life, sign me up!

"Good morning," he says sleepily, leaning forward to kiss me.

He tastes like peppermint.

"Morning," I say. "Want a bagel?"

"Sure. I'm going to scramble some eggs, too," he says, opening the fridge door, "and make bacon. Do you want some?"

"If you're cooking, yes."

I watch Jonah gather the eggs and a skillet and spatula. He cracks the eggs into a bowl and whisks them like a boss. I can't take my eyes off his half-naked body... his broad shoulders, his biceps, his back as it tapers down to his waist. His muscles flex and ripple beneath his tawny skin as he works.

Unable to resist, I walk up behind him as he stands at the stove, supervising breakfast. I slide my hands down his sides, past his waist to his hips. I grip them firmly, and he makes a rough sound deep in his chest. Then I wrap my arms around his waist, clasping my hands in front of his abs, and lay my head against his back. "I could get used to this. I mean, it's a definite perk if we're going to spend the rest of our lives together."

He turns in my arms and wraps his around my shoulders. "I'm glad you think so, because *newsflash*: we *are* going to spend the rest of our lives together."

"Speaking of news... Beth invited us upstairs to the penthouse for lunch today. She says they have *news.*"

Jonah lifts a brow. "Great. We have news, too."

"That's what I told her."

He grins, suddenly looking eager. "Are you ready for a public announcement? We don't have to, if you're not ready. We can keep this to ourselves for a while. It's up to you. But if you ask me, I vote yes. I want to tell everyone."

I gaze at my ring, liking the way it looks on my finger. It's discrete, not too ostentatious. It wouldn't get in the way during a fist fight. "We might as well tell them. They'll see the ring anyway."

He smiles, clearly pleased, and kisses me again. "Good."

* * *

At noon, we head up to the penthouse floor to join Beth and Shane for lunch. I assume Sam and Cooper will be there, too, as they share the penthouse. And of course Baby Luke. Sheesh. My brother's baby is freakishly adorable with his tufts of blond hair and bright blue eyes.

It seems like babies are sprouting up in my family like weeds. First Shane and Beth have one, and now Jake has a new step-son, and he and Annie are expecting. And I have a feeling my brother Jamie and his girlfriend are feeling their biological clocks ticking. Shoot, I don't ever need to have kids. I can just borrow my brothers' kids.

As we ride up in the private elevator, I glance down at the ring on my finger. It looks innocent enough. There aren't any flames shooting out of it. I'm sure Beth will notice, though, and then there'll be all kinds of *questions*. I hate questions.

When the elevator doors open, we step out into the foyer that leads into my brother's swanky apartment. Jonah opens the door and motions me through, and he follows me into the great room.

Shane is pacing barefoot in the open space between the sitting area and the kitchen, dressed in a pair of gray sweats and a navy blue T-shirt. There's a white burp cloth slung over his shoulder, and he's holding Luke to his chest, patting the baby's back. Luke doesn't seem impressed—he's squirming and squeaking.

"Hey, guys," Shane says, giving us a welcoming nod. "Glad you could make it."

My brother looks a bit harried at the moment as he bounces Luke in his arms. This is definitely out of character for my usually un-flappable big brother. But he's a first-time dad, so I guess it's to be expected.

"What's wrong with him?" I ask, watching the baby squirm.

"Nothing life-threatening," Shane says, attempting to placate the little wriggle worm. "Beth just nursed him, and I'm trying to get him to burp."

"Where is princess?" I say, glancing around the open floor plan for my sister-in-law.

"She's getting dressed. She'll be right out."

"Hey, squirt!" comes a deep, gravelly voice from the kitchen. "Glad you could make it."

I glance across the way at Cooper, who's flipping a steak on the indoor gas grill. Damn, lunch smells good. My stomach growls. "Hey, Coop."

"Make yourselves at home," Shane says, continuing with the pac-ing and the patting. "We'll be eating shortly. We're just waiting on

Beth and Sam."

Shane tosses the burp cloth over my shoulder. "Here, hold Luke while I go check on Beth." He hands me the baby.

My heart stutters painfully. "Shit, Shane, I don't know how to hold a baby."

He laughs as he hovers a moment, making sure I've got a secure hold on his son. "It's about time you learned. It's easy. Don't squeeze him too hard and, for God's sake, don't drop him. Other than that, you really can't mess up."

Afraid I will drop him, I clutch Luke to my chest. I have one hand propped beneath his diapered butt, and the other hand cradles his head and back, like I've seen Beth and Shane do. I must be doing it wrong, though, because Luke complains loudly, his innocuous little squeaks turning into full-blown squawks.

Jonah stands beside me, grinning like an idiot as he pats the baby's back. "You're doing great, tiger."

"I don't think he likes me!" I call after my brother, who's halfway down the hall to the suite he shares with his wife. "Shit, Shane! Don't leave me with him!"

"Watch your language in front of the baby, Lia," Cooper says as he pulls a tray of foil-wrapped baked potatoes out of the oven. "Let's not corrupt him prematurely."

Jonah steps in front of me. "Don't worry. You're doing great." He gently strokes Luke's hair, seemingly mesmerized by the kid.

"Don't you dare get ideas," I tell him, glaring at him over the kid's head.

Jonah grins at me, looking innocent. "I have no idea what you're talking about." Then he leans in to kiss the top of the baby's head. "He smells good. Smell him."

"I'm not going to smell him!" I say, bouncing the squirming kid in my arms. Luke's cries escalate quickly. "Seriously, I don't think he likes me."

Sam walks into the room, dressed in a pair of ripped jeans and a dark gray tee that has a rainbow on it, along with the words *Gay AF*. "Babies have good taste, you know," he says, taking Luke from me. "They're a good judge of character."

"Ha ha, Sam," I say, scowling at him. "You're so funny."

Sam cradles Luke in his arms, smiling down as he rocks the baby. "Hey, little fella," he croons in a gentle voice. "Was scary Auntie Lia being mean to you?" Immediately, the baby quiets. Sam raises his gaze to me. "See?"

I roll my eyes. "Oh, please. You are not The Baby Whisperer."

Beth walks into the great room, followed closely by Shane, who's wearing a white button-down shirt and shoes.

Beth's face lights up when she sees me. "Lia!"

She makes a beeline for me and wraps me in her arms. Then she smiles at Jonah. "I'm so glad you guys are here."

Princess looks happy and relaxed, dressed in a pale green sundress and flat white sandals. Her blonde hair is pulled up into a ponytail, and her smile is genuine.

I'm relieved to see her doing so well. Two months ago, she was struggling seriously with post-partum depression and fear for her premature son. I can't believe it's been two months since the traumatic delivery—an experience we shared together. Beth and I have always been close, but that experience forged an unbreakable bond between us. I helped her bring her son into the world under far from ideal conditions.

Beth holds my hands as she studies me. "How are you?" It's not just a casual question. She really cares.

I shrug. "I'm good. No complaints."

Her blue-green eyes catch on the gold band on my finger, her eyes widening. But she doesn't say anything. At least not yet. Instead, she turns her gaze to Jonah. "Hi, Jonah. How's everything?"

"Great," he says. "I'm almost finished with a new song."

"Oh, good! I can't wait to hear it. Send me an mp3 when it's ready?"

"Lunch is served!" Cooper calls, as he carries a platter of thick steaks to the table.

Beth rushes forward to help. Jonah and I grab cold drinks from the fridge. Sam takes a seat at the table, holding Luke in the crook of his arm. The baby's sleeping now, his tiny fist pressed against his cheek.

Beth leans over Sam's shoulder and brushes her fingers lightly across Luke's head. "Do you want me to take him? So you can eat?" she says.

"Nah, I'm good," Sam says. "You relax and enjoy your meal."

Shane pulls out a chair for Beth, then he takes a seat beside her.

The table is spread with an impressive feast, steaks, baked potatoes, roasted veggies, salad, and rolls.

"So," Shane says, eyeing me and Jonah as he cuts a piece off his steak. "Jake tells me you guys are interested in the single story house."

I freeze, trying not to choke on a mouthful of food.

Jonah lays his hand on my back, rubbing gently. "We looked at it Friday evening," he says. "Lia says she likes it."

I can't help noticing that everyone over the age of two months is staring at *me*. "What?" I say, after swallowing my food.

"Nothing," my brother says. "I'm just happy to hear you like the house."

I shrug. "Well, I've seen worse. Jonah likes it. I guess that's what matters. He'll be able to work from home, and we can minimize fiascos like the one last night at Rowdy's." I take a swig of my drink. "I can't believe you bought the entire subdivision."

Now it's Shane's turn to shrug. "It's a wise investment. Our family is growing, and especially with the influx of children, we need a safe place for them to reside. It just makes sense."

"What about you guys?" Jonah asks, looking at Shane, then Beth. "Are you going to live there, too?"

"We haven't decided," Shane says, glancing at his wife. "We're not quite ready to leave the penthouse, and Luke's still so young. But we'll have to make a change eventually, when he's more mobile."

"What about the lovebirds?" I say, eyeing first Cooper, then Sam. It wasn't that long ago that Cooper proposed to Sam at Rowdy's of all places, in front of our friends and family. "Don't you guys want a home of your own? A little... privacy?"

Sam blushes as he meets Cooper's gaze.

Cooper looks nonplussed. "It might have come up in discussion a time or two. But like Shane and Beth, we're not ready to do anything right away. We're happy here. And, it's best if Sam is close to Beth."

That makes perfect sense since Sam is Beth's full-time bodyguard, and now Luke's too, by association.

After lunch, Beth, Jonah, and I clean up the kitchen and put the dirty plates in the dishwasher. Shane disappears into his office to take a call. Sam and Cooper snuggle with Luke on one of the sofas.

"So," Beth says, when Jonah heads back to the table to collect more dirty dishes. She grins at me.

"What?" I reply, scowling. A flush creeps up my neck and into my cheeks. I know where this is going.

Her gaze goes to my left hand. "I noticed you're wearing a ring. It's lovely."

I shrug as I put dishes in the dishwasher. "It's just a ring. It's no big deal."

Beth glances at Jonah, who's still out of earshot. "Is it an engagement ring?"

"I guess."

She smiles. "Congratulations, Lia! I'm so happy for you both."

Jonah walks back into the kitchen carrying several glasses, which he sets on the countertop. "Thank you, Beth," he says, not bothering to hide the fact that he was eavesdropping. Then he takes me in his arms and kisses me. "I finally got her to say... 'all right, fine.'" He laughs.

Shane walks into the kitchen. "All right, fine, what?"

Jonah takes hold of my left hand and lifts it up for Shane to see. "Your sister and I are engaged."

Shane's eyes widen as he looks right at me. "Really?" he says, not taking Jonah at his word. When I nod, his face lights up. "Lia, congratulations!" he says. "Have you told Mom and Dad?"

"God, no. You're the first ones we've told."

My big brother pulls me into a bear hug and squeezes tight. Then he kisses the top of my head. "I'm happy for you, sis."

I absolutely hate being the center of attention, but Jonah looks pleased, so I grin and bear it.

At that moment, Luke erupts in a breathy wail across the room, and Cooper stands, bouncing the baby in his arms. "Mama," he says. "You're needed."

Beth smiles as she lays down a dishtowel. "Coming!" she calls. And then to us, she says, "That's my cue." She presses her hand to her breasts. "Right on time because I'm about to start leaking." Then she heads toward Cooper, who meets her halfway to hand her the baby.

Shane follows Beth to the nursery, and Cooper turns on the TV to check baseball scores. The Chicago Cubs are playing at Wrigley Field.

A sense of contentment washes over me. Shane and Beth are deliriously happy with their new baby boy. Sam and Cooper seem quite happy. Jonah and I are moving... forward? I'm suddenly liking the idea of playing house with him... in a real house.

As I twist the gold band on my ring finger, Jonah moves behind me and wraps his arms around my waist, leaning down to rest his chin on my shoulder. He turns his mouth toward me and whispers in my ear. "I can't wait for us to move into our new house. We'll have to christen every single room, every surface."

I laugh. "We have to buy the house first."

He tightens his arms around me. "That's just a formality. I'll call the bank tomorrow. We should be able to move in this week. And then we can christen every room." He kisses the side of my neck, sending a shiver down my spine.

When Beth and Shane return a short while later, holding a happy baby Luke, Jonah holds out his hands. "Can I hold him?"

"Sure," Beth says, smiling as she gently lays her son in Jonah's arms.

Jonah looks at me, grinning as he cradles the baby to his chest.

"Jonah Locke, don't you dare get any ideas," I tell him, shaking my head vehemently. "You got your way with the ring and the house. Don't push your luck, pal."

# Epilogue

## Jonah Locke

I'm feeling pretty content as I watch Lia hang her clothes up in our new closet. *In our new house.*

Our furniture's been moved in, the kitchen stocked. Work on the recording studio is scheduled to begin in a week, and Lia's fitness equipment has already been ordered. Everything's coming together perfectly.

Jake and Annie have already moved into their new house across the street from us. I think Aiden has run back and forth between our houses half a dozen times in excitement, crossing the street under the watchful eyes of his new daddy. There's virtually no traffic on the two-lane street dividing our houses, as all construction has ceased for the moment. Lia's parents—Calum and Bridget—are moving into the house beside Jake's, and Ingrid, Beth's mom, has accepted Shane's offer of a home here as well. She's been working with an architect to choose her floorplan.

I think it's only a matter of time before Beth and Shane decide to move here, too, along with Sam and Cooper.

"Do you like your house?" Aiden asks, as he walks into our bedroom.

I'm sitting on our bed, waiting for Lia to finish up in the closet. Aiden jumps up on the bed and sits beside me, swinging his legs. Stevie is tucked beneath his arm.

"I like it a lot," I tell him. "How about you? Do you like your new house?"

"Oh, yeah!" His face lights up. "I got a new bed. It looks like a race car!"

"Cool. I can't wait to see it."

"Aiden!"

"That's my daddy!" Aiden says, hopping off the bed. "In here, Daddy! In the bedroom!"

Jake parks himself in the open doorway, leaning against the door jamb as he peers around the room. "Where's Lia?"

"She's hanging up her clothes," Aiden says, pointing toward the closet.

Jake nods. "I came to collect you, young man. It's time for dinner."

"Aww," Aiden says, pouting. "I want to stay and visit Aunt Lia and Uncle Jonah."

"Later, pal," Jake says, motioning Aiden to come forward. "It's time for your dinner."

"Okay." Aiden hops off the bed and heads for the door. He tosses back a wave to me. "See you later, Uncle Jonah."

I return the gesture. "See you later, buddy."

When Lia comes out of the closet, she looks around. "Are we alone?"

"Yes. Jake came to get Aiden for dinner."

She nods. "Good. Stay right there." She leaves our room, and I wonder where she's gone. She returns a few moments later, whipping her tee off as she walks into our room.

I'm treated to the sight of her beautiful breasts cradled in a black bra. As she walks toward me, she reaches back to unfasten her bra, letting the fabric fall unceremoniously to the floor.

"You said we need to christen every room," she says, pushing me back on the mattress and climbing on top of me.

So far we've christened the kitchen and the home office, but we're still working our way through the house. Counting the lower level, there are twelve more rooms to go.

She prowls over me like a panther, hungry and determined. Damn, it's such a turn-on when she gets like this. My hands automatically go to her waist, and I gently stroke her warm skin. Her breasts hover over my face, radiating heat. God, she smells so good. My dick hardens in response.

"What if Aiden pops in again without warning?" I say, already breathing hard. The kid's been in and out of our house all afternoon.

"I locked the doors." She leans down and kisses me, her mouth hot and eager. "If he comes back, he'll have to ring the bell."

Her tongue slips inside and teases mine, making my pulse hammer and my head spin. Then she reaches between us and unsnaps my jeans, unzipping them and tugging them halfway down my thighs.

My eyes roll back into my head, and I find myself at the mercy of her mouth, which is as heavenly as it is snarky. She has the ability to unravel me like no one else.

"Welcome home, Mr. Locke," she says, proceeding to blow my mind.

I think I'm going to like home ownership.

I have a secret, three-part plan.

First, get her to wear my ring. Check.

Second, get her into a house. Check.

And lastly, well... I'd better not push my luck right now.

Not while I'm ahead.

*The end... for now.*

# Books by April Wilson

**McIntyre Security, Inc. Bodyguard Series:**

*Vulnerable*

*Fearless*

*Shane (a novella)*

*Broken*

*Shattered*

*Imperfect*

*Ruined*

*Hostage*

*Redeemed*

*Marry Me (a novella)*

*Snowbound (a novella)*

*Regret*

*With This Ring (a novella)*

*Collateral Damage*

**A Tyler Jamison Novel:**

*Somebody to Love*

*Somebody to Hold*

**A British Billionaire Romance:**

*Charmed* (co-written with Laura Riley)

**Audiobooks by April Wilson**

For links to my audiobooks, please visit my website:
www.aprilwilsonauthor.com/audiobooks

# Coming Next!

Stay tuned for more books featuring your favorite McIntyre Security characters! Watch for upcoming books for Tyler Jamison, Sophie McIntyre, Charlie, Killian and Hannah McIntyre, Cameron and Chloe, Liam McIntyre, Ingrid Jamison, and many more!

# Please Leave a Review on Amazon

I hope you'll take a moment to leave a review for me on Amazon. Please, please, please? It doesn't have to be long... just a brief comment saying whether you liked the book or not. Reviews are vitally important to authors! I'd be incredibly grateful to you if you'd leave one for me. Goodreads and BookBub are also great places to leave reviews.

# Stay in Touch

Follow me on Facebook or subscribe to my newsletter for up-to-date information on the schedule for new releases. You'll find my website at www.aprilwilsonauthor.com.

I'm active daily on Facebook, and I love to interact with my readers. Come talk to me on Facebook by leaving me a message or a comment. Please share my book posts with your friends. I also have a very active reader group on Facebook where I post weekly teasers for new books and run lots of giveaway contests. Just search for **April Wilson Reader Fan Club**. Come join us!

You can also follow me on Amazon, BookBub, Goodreads, and Instagram!

Made in the USA
Columbia, SC
14 May 2024